THE
SUPERNATURAL
SOCIETY
CURSE OF THE WEREWOLVES

Books by Rex Ogle
available from Inkyard Press

The Supernatural Society
Curse of the Werewolves

THE SUPERNATURAL SOCIETY
CURSE OF THE WEREWOLVES

.sterces sah dik yrevE

esehT eerht era gninrael srieht era erom gniyfirret naht tsom.

REX OGLE

inkyard PRESS

ISBN-13: 978-1-335-91583-2

Curse of the Werewolves

Inkyard Press
22 Adelaide St. West, 41st Floor
Toronto, Ontario M5H 4E3, Canada
www.InkyardPress.com

Printed in U.S.A.

asiraM oT

…deid ohw…

seirots yracs ym syojne llits tub

.syas ehs os ro…

a second grave warning

To the human (or are you?) holding this book:

Did you see the cover of this book? Rex Ogle is once again attempting to take credit for my story. The nerve! Who does this creature think he is? I wrote this story—me, Adam Monster. Not ~~Same~~ some...some... Texan lumberdork who reads comics all day.

And ~~as~~ if that weren't bad enough, YOU have returned.

sigh

Did I or did I not warn you in the last book NOT to read my story, and also NOT to pursue this one? I most certainly did. Yet you are back... Tell me—and be honest—why would you want to put yourself through

~~the~~ this again? I assure you, this book is even more gruesome and ghastly and gross than the ~~last~~ last.

I would completely understand if you choose to stop reading right this second. ~~book.~~ After all, my life has already been filled with plenty of rejection. First my parents were mortified at my face, then they disowned me, casting me out into the wild of the world. Upon seeing me, girls often say, "What a wretched face you have!" Boys often say, "What awful clothes you wear!" Dogs often bark, "What an awful stench you have!" And more than one monster says, "What a terrible temper you have! Why are you trying to ~~kill~~ ax murder me? Is it because I ate those children?"

(The ~~the~~ answer is yes. I am a monster, but I do not condone eating children...most of the time.)

So please, go ahead. ~~alphabet.~~ Abandon me as so many others have. I do not mind. What's one more person pretending not to know me?

Go on. Ditch this book. Drop it in a landfill. Drown it in the ocean. Or better yet, feed it to a coyote or a bear ~~and~~ or a lion. If you have the means, shoot it into outer space. Or, if you are conscientious of the planet, simply recycle the paper. Saving trees is quite noble, and I fully support it.

Whatever you do, do NOT ~~find~~ read any further.

...

Criminy! Why are you still reading?! Perhaps a bullet point list will help reason with your rebellious nature and aid ~~the~~ my argument:

#1. Because I am a MONSTER. Thus the only ~~secret~~ stories I know are MONSTROUS.

#2. Because this story will teach you nothing, and then your parents and teachers will be angry with you for not spending this time learning MATH. Math is useful. This story is NOT.

#3. Because the following chapters contain ~~message~~ MONSTERS, MYTHS, MAGIC, and MAD SCIENCE—which means if you do not find it mundane, then you will be panicky unnerved, upset, distressed, and of course, TERRIFIED.

Do you really want that?
What do you mean, "yes!"?!
double sigh
I am NOT going to beg you.
...

Okay, fine. I am on my hands and knees begging, pleading with you... Please please please please

please please please please please please PLEASE do NOT read this book. If you do, you'll be stuck reading it forever...in your GRAVE.

What are you giggling at? Cut that out!

I can see there is no talking you out of it. You are a glutton for punishment. If you cannot sleep tonight because of the nightmares, do NOT call me. I tried to warn you.

Sincerely, and WORST,
yours darkly,

-Adam Monster

p.s.

Oanbcced aegfagihni, Ij hkalvmen foiplqlresdt
muyv twaxlyez

waibtchd ceofdgehsi, cjikplhmenrosp, aqnrds
ctruyvpwtxoygzraabmcsd.

Deofng'th biej skclamrneodp. Yqorus'vteu gvowtx
tyhziasb.

You're welcome.

-Adam Monster

Chapter 1
under a full moon

Will's life was over.

No, he was not dead—*yet*—but it felt like everything was ending. And that feeling threatened to overwhelm him. Of course, that's what happens when you find out you've been bitten by a *werewolf*.

Dear Reader, I am getting ahead of myself, aren't I? You need some setup for our story to begin. Apologies. Let me clear my throat of phlegm and spiders, then I'll start over…

Ahem!

Ew. Those weren't spiders in my throat. They were maggots.

💀 💀 💀

It was the second day of November when Will Hunter walked home after school with new friends Ivy and Linus.

The adopted siblings were talking and laughing, but Will's mind was occupied elsewhere. He waved a "See ya later" before jogging inside. He pulled out his mom's cell phone and tried to call his dad for the 128th time. He waited impatiently as the phone rang. And rang. And rang again. And again. And again. Until:

"You've reached the voice mail of Mr. Henry Hunter. Please leave a message at the beep." *Beep!*

"Dad. It's Will…again. I was calling because…um, I wanted to say hi, I guess. We haven't talked since I moved to the island of East Emerson. It's only been a month, but it feels like…like a really long time. I know you and Mom aren't speaking because of the…the d-i-v-o-r-c-e, but that doesn't mean *we* can't talk. Right? Um…am I gonna get to see you for Thanksgiving? Since Mom can barely cook, you always said it was *our* holiday." Will smiled at the memory, of him and his dad spending hours in the kitchen, making pumpkin pie and turkey and stuffing and mashed potatoes and green beans, which were boiled for hours with bacon to make them soft and salty… "Turkey Day is only three weeks away. Are you…coming here? Or could I…I don't know…maybe come see you? Just, uh…can you call me back? Please."

Will didn't know what else to say. He ended the call.

He held Mom's cell phone in both of his hands for several minutes. He wondered, if he wished hard enough, would his dad call back? He stood there for a long time, trying to will the phone to ring.

It did not.

Will's stomach grew heavy, like he'd swallowed a bunch of rocks. It felt like the room was spinning, like he might puke. So he took off his backpack, letting it slide to the kitchen's linoleum floor. He lay down beside it. It seemed odd to lie down in the middle of the room, but for whatever reason, it made his anxiety lessen.

Will tried to focus on his breathing like his friends had taught him.

A few minutes later, a large, wet tongue licked his face. "I'm okay, Fitz," Will lied to his dog. The Saint Bernard knew better. With a quiet whimper, Fitz lay down next to his best friend, resting his head on Will's chest. The two stayed there for a long time.

Eventually, Fitz got up and walked out of the room, then returned a few moments later with a video game controller in his mouth. The dog dropped it into Will's lap.

"You always know what I need," Will said, scratching Fitz behind the ears. Will went to the living room couch and turned on the TV. Playing video games helped lift his spirits—at least until his mom, Ms. Vásquez, came home from her job at the hospital.

"Is your homework done, mijo?"

"No, but I'll do it later."

"Video games *off*. Homework *on*," said Ms. Vásquez.

"What's the point?" Will mumbled. "Getting good grades isn't going to make Dad come back."

"¿Perdóneme?" Mom asked.

"Nothing," Will said. He tossed the game controller on the coffee table and started storming up the stairs.

"Guillermo Hunter. Do *not* walk away from me like that."

"My name is *Will*," he snapped. Though technically, *Guillermo* was on his birth certificate. It meant the same as *William*, and Dad always called him *Will*. But Dad wasn't here.

"Please. Talk to me, mijo," Mom said earnestly. She was sitting on the couch in her nursing scrubs, her hands cupped together. She looked tired and sad, which opened up another ache inside Will.

Ms. Vásquez got up, crossed to the stairs, and took her son's hand. "I know the divorce has been hard. We had to leave Brooklyn, you had to leave Marcellus and your friends, we had to move to a new town. It's a lot of change, and change can be scary—"

Scary? Will thought of all the things he had seen since moving to East Emerson: vampires, zombies, giant spiders, razor-toothed mermaids, underground tunnels with a heartbeat, terrible messages decoded with a golden pyramid key, a witch that had tried to kill him and his new friends… The word *scary* didn't begin to cover it.

"—but change can also be good," Mom finished.

"What's good about Dad forgetting me?" Will asked.

His mom squeezed her lips together. "He hasn't forgotten you, Will. He could never do that."

"Then I guess he just forgot how to use a phone," Will said, pulling his hand free. "That must be why he hasn't returned my calls."

Will stomped up the stairs to his room. When he slammed the door, the photos on the walls shook.

Dear Reader, I know you think Will is a punk, a brat, and a bit of a turd. Though he is certainly *behaving* like a punk, a brat, and a bit of a turd, he is *not* any of these things. Do not judge him too harshly. Sometimes, life gives each of us an obstacle to overcome—one that will make us lash out at those we love, be they mothers, friends, or neighbors.

That is what Will is doing: lashing out. His anger is eating him up inside. But he isn't really angry with his mom. He's angry at his dad. Despite his turd-like behavior, my heart aches for Will. It is never fun when your feelings are hurt, especially by a parent.

It is also not fun when someone stabs you with a pitchfork or sets you on fire. Both of these things have happened to me—many times, actually. But neither of those things hurt quite as much as my own parents abandoning me. When parents—the very people who brought us into this world—hurt us, it can leave horribly deep wounds. And right now, Will's wounds were still fresh after his father's departure…

After Will slammed the door, he threw himself onto his bed and hid his face in the pillow, trying to will himself not to cry.

💀💀💀

When Will finally got up, his eyes burned and his throat was raw. The sun had set, and he could smell Mom cooking downstairs. The salty scent meant hot dogs—which, Hungry Reader, I recently learned are *not* made of actual dogs, but of *pigs*. You might think me ridiculous, but shouldn't these tasty meat tubes be called *hot pigs* instead?

Where was I? Oh, yes…

Will stopped at the kitchen threshold. "Sorry," he whispered to his mom, "about earlier. I'm not mad at you."

"I know," Ms. Vásquez said. She wiped her hands on a kitchen towel, then hugged her son. She kissed him on the forehead. "Siéntate. Dinner's ready. I'm sorry it's hot dogs and mac 'n' cheese again, but I don't get my first paycheck until next week."

"It's okay," Will said. Though secretly, he didn't like being broke.

As they ate, Mom told Will about her day. "…and then I said, I don't think I can change another catheter. Seven is enough for one shift, thank you very much! Do you know where a catheter goes?"

Will did. He scrunched his face and waved his arms. "Stop, Mom! That is *not* dinner conversation."

"Then tell me about your day."

"The usual. Walked to school with Ivy and Linus, went to class, had lunch, went to more classes."

"I'm so glad you're making friends."

"Two friends," Will said. "But yeah, they are pretty great."

Mom pointed her fork at Will. "How did your math test go?"

"It was canceled. Mr. Villalobos couldn't stop scratching

and sneezing and blowing his nose. He could barely write on the board. He said it's just monthly allergies. Apparently, he's allergic to dogs, which is hilarious because Mr. Villalobos is a *werewolf*. Can you believe it? He's allergic to himself!"

Ms. Vásquez sighed. "Will, these strange little stories are very creative—but I don't think you should make up things about your teachers."

Except Will was *not* making up stories. He was telling the truth. East Emerson was a beautiful beach town with piers and lighthouses and salt in the air. But it was also a strange town with strange happenings—the least of which was a werewolf math teacher. Ms. Vásquez did not know that. A town curse kept everyone from seeing monsters. When they did notice something strange, they immediately forgot or stopped thinking about it. Will and his friends were the few exceptions. Will's mom was not so lucky—if that's what you call lucky.

Will hated lying to his mom. Even though he had no choice *but* to lie after she made him promise to stop talking about the monsters, magic, myths, and mad science that he saw in this new town. So he tried not to bring it up, but sometimes—like just now—he accidentally told the truth.

"Sorry," Will said. He shoved the last bite of dog and bun

into his mouth, smearing yellow mustard across his cheek. He took his mom's plate and his own and washed the dishes. Fitz followed him to the sink and started growling.

Will looked outside the window. A hare sat on a tree branch, watching him.

This wasn't just any hare, Smart Reader. After all, this is East Emerson, where the weirdest of weird lives and breathes. This hare had a red cybernetic eye, an antenna, different-colored arms and legs stitched together like a doll, and tiny dragon wings. Its name was Faust, and it belonged to a rather wicked witch named Ozzie.

For the last two days, the patchwork hare had been watching Will and his friends. Whenever Faust showed its whiskers, they pretended not to see it. They didn't want the witch to know Will and Ivy remembered what happened after she had tried to erase their memories...

The phone rang. Will raced to answer it. "Dad?"

"Uh, no, it's Ivy. Remember me? The Korean girl who lives across the street?"

"Yeah, I know who you are," Will whispered. "Hey."

"Wow. Don't be too happy to hear from me," Ivy said. "Anyways, have you looked out your window? It's a full moon."

"So?"

"The magic fox's warning. Remember? The silver fox that talks and gives us cryptic messages in rhymes about how we can save the town? Get over here. We have work to do."

Outside the window, the hare flew off into the night sky, passing briefly in front of the full moon. Will took a deep breath. Anything was better than waiting for his dad to call—even throwing himself into danger. "I'm on my way." Will dried his hands, then shoved his shoes on. "Mom, I'm running across the street to hang with Linus and Ivy."

"Be home before ten," Mom called after him.

Will jogged across Ophidian Drive. A Korean girl and a Black boy waited at their front door. Ivy wore her usual ball cap along with a soccer jersey and sweatpants cut into shorts. Linus wore loafers, ironed pants, and a crisp white button-up shirt. He pushed his glasses up his nose.

Ivy scanned the sky before whispering, "Did you get a visit from Franken-Hare too?"

"Faust? Yeah, I saw it spying on me."

Linus huffed. "I would like to see this flying creature as well."

Ivy rolled her eyes. "Yeah, but you can't. You just have to trust us for now. You know that Will and I have magic sight that lets us see all the weird, wild stuff."

"I am aware," Linus stated. "You have a magic ring. And Will is just…well, statistically and improbably lucky?"

"More like cursed," Will whispered. He didn't know why he could see what most could not. He wondered if he was born like this…or if maybe his dad could see stuff too… He wished his father would return his calls.

"Still, if I am to be a valuable asset to this team, I need to be able to see through the town curse as well, don't I?" Linus crossed his arms. "As a man of science, I prefer to perceive things with my own two eyes rather than trust my sister, who pranks me almost every morning."

Ivy snorted with laughter. "Oh, man. Today's was hilarious. I put plastic wrap on the toilet seat, and—"

"Moving on!" Linus snapped. "It is a full moon, and we should—"

A deep, horrible howl filled the night air. The streets of their neighborhood seemed darker than usual, despite being well lit by the bright, massive moon in the sky.

Linus said, "Let us retire to my room to continue our conversation on the unfolding of East Emerson's eerie events—especially in light of tonight's lunar situation."

As Ivy waved him in, Will realized he'd never been inside their house before. The Cross home looked like something out of a magazine. The furniture was sleek and modern, each item having its own place and every surface as clean as a whistle. It made Will's stomach twist into knots. He and his mom were still living out of the cardboard boxes they had moved here in last month.

As the three friends walked toward the carpeted stairs, Mr. Cross popped his head out from the kitchen. "Hey, Will. Settling in across the street alright?"

"Yes, sir."

"Did you already have dinner? We have leftover vegetable lasagna if you're hungry."

"I just ate, but thank you."

"Do you kids want dessert?" Mr. Cross added. "Will, have you ever had nurungji? It's crispy rice sprinkled with sugar. We also have lemon–cream cheese pound cake."

"Dad, stop! We're fine," Ivy groaned. She rolled her eyes, muttering under her breath, "So annoying. Just because we're adopted doesn't mean you have to try so hard."

Will didn't understand Ivy's attitude. Her father was so nice and…present.

"I can't help it if my world revolves around my children," Mr. Cross said. "You're only the two most amazing kids in the world. No offense, Will."

"None taken," Will said.

"Whatever." Ivy grabbed Will's arm and dragged him upstairs behind Linus. "Come on, Will. We have stuff to do."

Huge shelves lined Linus's bedroom, each overflowing with books. His large desk held two computers, a microscope, various rocks in beakers and jars, several journals filled with notes, and a glass ball with blue electricity dancing around inside. Pointing out the window was a high-powered telescope. A framed poster on the wall showed Albert Einstein sticking his tongue out.

On the bed, Linus's massive backpack lay open. Every pocket and compartment was filled, perfectly organized to fit an impossible number of items: flashlights, a Swiss Army knife, multi-tools, pens, a first aid kit, a hand-crank radio, extra batteries, snacks, a bottle of water, a can of Mace spray, tape, an emergency whistle, binoculars, a magnifying glass, moist towelettes, a pair of pantyhose…

Pantyhose? Will was about to ask when Linus answered, "I make sure my go bag contains everything for *any* eventuality in an emergency situation. After our lack of batteries on our last quest, I realized I needed to amp up my preparation game. But we are not here to discuss that. We have a mystery to solve. Have a seat." Linus closed his backpack and offered two beanbags to his guests. "I have come up with a three-step proposition to save our town."

Linus flipped over a dry-erase board. It said:

LINUS'S PLAN OF ATTACK
#1—Discover Ozzie's Motive & Plans
#2—Stop Ozzie's Plans & Save the Town
#3—Hand Ozzie Over to the Authorities

"Wow. That's so simple. Why didn't I think of that?" Ivy said sarcastically. "Seriously, Linus. You think bagging Ozzie—an ancient and powerful witch who can kill us with the snap of her magic fingers—is going to be that easy? Puh-leaze."

"I admit my initial strategy is uncomplicated, but we need to commence somewhere," Linus said. "Currently, our only lead is a fox's riddle."

Will repeated the rhyme. "'Beware the full moon and hirsute strangers. East Emerson is still full of dangers.'"

"And tonight's the full moon," Ivy said.

"Precisely why we agreed to gather this evening," Linus added. "So let us dissect this little riddle. According to the *Farmers' Almanac*, the first full moon of November is called the Beaver Moon."

Ivy laughed. "You think we're going to be fighting bea-vers?"

"Is that any stranger than vampire pets?" Linus asked.

"That's fair," Ivy said. "Back to the riddle. Beware strang-ers? Every little kid knows that. So we don't get in vans with creeps offering us candy. That's easy. What's *hair-suit* mean, though?"

"Hirsute," Linus corrected. "It means 'hairy.'"

"Hairy strangers?" Ivy scrunched up her face like she'd stepped in dog doo. "Gross."

"I have been considering the parallel between phrases *full moon* and *hirsute strangers*," Linus noted, "and I have a hypothesis: lycanthropes."

"Like-can-*what*?" Ivy asked.

"Lycanthropes. Another word for *werewolves*," Linus said. "Unfortunately, such things are not real—are they?"

"This is East Emerson," Ivy said. "Everything supernatu-ral is real here."

"My math teacher, Mr. Villalobos, is a werewolf," Will said. "But he's really nice. And I'm not sure if he counts as a stranger."

Ivy paced the room. "In October, we fought vampires. Now we're going up against werewolves? That's so—"

"—scary?" Will finished.

"—frightening?" Linus asked.

"—rad!" Ivy smirked. "Let's go on patrol. See if we can spot anything."

"I prefer to have a plan," Linus noted.

"Plan-*schman*," Ivy said. "We just need to go outside and look for hairy strangers."

"I agree with Ivy." Will shrugged. "It's a small town. Maybe just a lap or two on our bikes. We might notice something."

"Yeah," Ivy said. "What's the worst that could happen?"

Dear Reader, please make a mental note for you and your loved ones to never utter the words *What's the worst that could happen?* Saying these words is like an invitation to the universe to make *the worst* happen. No one wants the worst. Perhaps try saying *What's* the best *that could happen?* Wouldn't you rather something *best* happen than something *worst*?

Will, Ivy, and Linus nodded to one another. Adventure was calling to them, and they could not resist answering. Linus grabbed his backpack, then they raced down the stairs.

"Going out?" Mr. Cross said, holding a sheet of freshly baked chocolate chip cookies. "I was making you a treat."

"Sorry, Dad," Ivy said, snatching one and shoving it in her mouth. "Ow! Hot! Gotta run! Last-minute homework assignment."

"But it's almost nine—"

"That is correct," Linus said. "You see, our, uh, science professor asked us to record our observations of the effects a full moon has on fireflies. Best done after dark."

"Oh, okay. Have fun. Be careful," Mr. Cross said. "Stay close to home!"

As Ivy and Linus rushed out the door, Will hesitated. His gut grew heavy as he thought of his own dad. "Thanks, Mr. Cross. Your kids are lucky to have you."

A few minutes later, Will was pedaling his bike alongside Linus and Ivy, who opted for a skateboard instead. Linus wiped sweat from his brow. "I cannot believe I manufactured an untruth to one of our parental units."

"You mean you lied! I'm so proud of you, little bro. Just another step on your road to being like me."

"I banish the thought," Linus said.

"Isn't your backpack a little heavy to lug around everywhere?" Will asked.

"Yes. But as the adage goes, 'it is preferrable to be secure than apologetic,'" Linus answered.

"He means 'better safe than sorry,'" Ivy noted.

"That is what I said," Linus snorted. "No matter what situation arises, I have something in this bag to provide aid."

"Are there gummy bears in there?" Ivy asked.

"There are," Linus said, "for emergencies only."

The friends rode their bikes and skateboard from the cemetery to the eastern lighthouse, then toward downtown. They rode past the bowling alley and ice cream shop, then toward the clock tower, the library, and the movie theater. They didn't see werewolves, but they did see other strange beings: a woman walking her dog, both of them ghosts. A coven of witches racing each other on broomsticks. A fire truck driven by several scowling snowmen. A father carrying groceries from his minivan to his house—he and his family all five-foot-tall ants. And at the traffic light, a man on a motorcycle rode up beside them—only the man had no head at all.

Not able to see what Will and Ivy saw, Linus called out, "Excuse me, sir? You really should wear a helmet when riding a two-wheeled motor vehicle."

The headless man made a rude gesture, then sped away when the light turned green.

"Did you see that?" Will asked Ivy.

"The Headless Horseman? Yeah, he's harmless. Last year, he sold his horse and upgraded to a Harley-Davidson."

"He was headless?" Linus groaned. Under his breath, he added, "I never see the fun stuff."

"It's getting late," Will noted. "I need to get home before ten."

"*Shhh*," Ivy whispered. "Do you hear that?"

"I do not hear a thing," Linus answered.

"Exactly," Ivy said. "No insect sounds of any kind. Strange, considering it's usually a cricket chorus every—"

"AH-WOOOOOOOOOOOO!"

The howl tore through the night. A shiver went up Will's spine. "Maybe we should head home," Will said. "I mean, we already saved the town once. Shouldn't we get some time off? I mean…we almost died. Ozzie was going to kill us if not for the gray-skinned stranger."

"But we *didn't* die," Ivy argued. "And we're not going up against Ozzie tonight. We're looking for hair-suit stranger danger."

"Hirsute," Linus corrected.

"Look, we came out, we looked around," Will said. "And it's nothing but the usual monsters, magic, myths, and mad science. If the silver fox really wanted us to do something, she would have given us more of a clue."

"But—" Ivy started.

Will interrupted, "Also, I don't want to get grounded. My mom would worry. So would your dad."

"Who cares about our dad?" Ivy sneered.

"Actually, I do," Linus said. "And so do you. Stop pretending, Ivy. Plus, I concur with our neighbor. We should head home."

"Fine," Ivy groaned. She hopped on her skateboard and led the way, mumbling complaints under her breath. Will and Linus followed on their bikes.

On Fang Lane, only four blocks from home, they noticed a bright red car—stenciled with letters spelling out NEIGHBORHOOD WATCH. Front doors wide-open, no driver in sight, it was parked outside a pink house. A little white flashing light on top of the car lit the quiet street, but no one was around. The trio slowed and stopped. "Uh. Where's the Neighborhood Watch people?" Will asked.

"Better question," Ivy said, pointing at the white fence across the street. "Is that one of Ozzie's coded messages?"

14-15-23 09-19 20-08-05 20-09-13-05:
19-20-01-18-20 02-09-20-09-14-07.
09 23-01-14-20 01-14 01-18-13-25 15-06 23-05-
18-05-23-15-12-22-05-19
<u>01-19-01-16.</u>

Will pulled the golden pyramid key out of his pocket. Ever since he'd found it in the vampire veterinarian's office, he hadn't let it out of his sight. But there were only letters on his pyramid, no numbers. Will forgot the code when he realized he was standing in something sticky. He whispered, "Don't look down."

Ivy and Linus, of course, looked down. The three kids were standing in a puddle of scarlet red, some of which was smeared over the sides of the Neighborhood Watch car. They started to back slowly away, when someone asked, "What are you doing?"

"*Arghh!*" the three young heroes shrieked. They turned to see a man and woman emerging from the shadows beside the pink house.

"O-M-G, dudes," Ivy gasped. "Don't sneak up on people like that."

"Sorry about that," the first man chuckled with a strange

smirk. He gave a friendly wave. "No need to be frightened. I'm Mr. Ramirez. I live down the street on Spiral Drive."

"And I'm Mrs. Maxwell," said the second person. "I live over on Redrum Way. Might we ask why you kids are out so late?"

"Just riding our bikes home after a late study session," Ivy lied with ease. "What happened here?"

"Nothing to concern yourselves with. Just a routine neighborhood patrol, making sure everyone is safe."

"And this pool of plasma?" Linus asked.

The Neighborhood Watch's smiles disappeared. Mr. Ramirez stepped more fully into the light of the full moon, revealing a torn pant leg and a bloody calf. "No big deal. Just a small accident."

"Small? It looks like you put your leg in a blender," Ivy said.

"Only an animal bite. It'll heal," Mr. Ramirez said.

"What kind of animal?" But even as Will asked, he saw similar wounds on Mrs. Maxwell's arm and neck...only the deep cuts were healing before his eyes. A few seconds later, all that was left were scars in the shape of a crescent moon and smears of dried red.

"Nothing to worry about. Just a spooked dog," Mrs. Maxwell answered. "Now, why don't you three hop in our car and we'll give you a ride home."

As Mr. Ramirez opened the back door, Will, Ivy, and Linus noticed the same thing: his arms grew hairier before their eyes. So did his face and hands. Then his eyes turned black. The same happened to Mrs. Maxwell.

As you may or may not know, Dear Reader, werewolves have quite the healing ability. I know from having tussled with such beasts during the War of the Oranges, a war which had little to do with the delicious fruit. Fortunately, my flesh is already cadaverous, so their wolfen bites did nothing more than annoy me. My point being, for a human—such as Will, Ivy, Linus, and presumably yourself—once bitten, you can transform into a wolf for the first time in a matter of mere minutes. If ever you come face-to-face with a lycanthrope, I suggest you run fast, Dear Reader—unless of course you enjoy howling at full moons and lifting your leg to pee.

"Uh, did you two have beards a second ago?" Ivy asked.

"They did not," Will answered. "But they do now."

Will's eyes grew as the two Neighborhood Watch members in front of him became even hairier. Low growls rumbled up from their chests as they began to gyrate, as if having seizures. Then their bodies made cracking sounds, like their bones were snapping and changing inside. They began to shape-shift.

"Linus, we have to get out of here," Ivy said.

"Why?" Linus asked, unable to see what Ivy and Will saw.

Mr. Ramirez growled. He burst from his clothes into a full man-size wolf. He leaped at Linus. Ivy jumped in the way, swinging her skateboard like a baseball bat. The board cracked in two over the wolf's face. "Stay away from my brother, hair-suit!"

"Ivy, you just hit the Neighborhood Watch!" Linus screeched.

"He's a werewolf!" Ivy shouted. "They're both werewolves!"

Linus rubbed his eyes and shook his head. Where he had seen two rather regular neighbors, now all he saw were two large wolves. But Will and Ivy—with their gift of magical sight—saw the truth: two hulking werewolves, salivating at the mouth.

"AH-WOOOOOOOOOO!" they howled.

"*Go! Go! Go!*" Ivy shouted. She leaped onto the back of Will's bike as he and Linus started pedaling. They'd already turned the street corner when Ivy looked back. The feral beasts were chasing them. She cried out, "Hurry!"

"I'm going as fast as I can!" Will shouted.

"Go faster! They're gaining!" she shouted. The bicycles

sped around one block and toward Ophidian Drive. "We have to get home. Werewolves can't get in without an invitation!"

"That is vampires!" Linus shouted. "Werewolves can go wherever they want."

"Then we *can't* go home," Will shouted. "Or we'll lead them straight to our parents."

"Where do we go then?!"

Will, Ivy, and Linus didn't know that they were all feeling the exact same thing at the exact same time—true, deep, and utter panic.

Though he would never admit it out loud, Linus trusted his sister. If she said werewolves were after them, then he knew they were in danger. Sweat beaded across his forehead and heat fogged his glasses.

Though she would *never* admit it out loud, Ivy loved her brother and would do anything to protect him. Her heart pounded against her chest as she tried to figure out a way to keep him safe.

And though he *would* admit it, Will hated that the only thing he could think about was that his dad didn't care if he lived or died. But Will wasn't going to die, Worried Reader. Not yet anyway.

A bird flew down from the sky, her feathers glowing

with the same radiant white as the moon. Dropping from above, she transformed into the silver fox and landed in the middle of the road. She pointed a front paw to the left, calling out, *"Do not hesitate, do not delay. Hurry up now, follow me this way."*

Will and Linus turned left, biking after the fox, who bounded into the air and transformed into a gleaming eagle. Ivy held on to Will's shoulders as she looked back. The werewolves were gaining. "Faster, boys. Pedal like your life depends on it—'cause it does."

The eagle led the kids away from the paved streets, toward the eastern woods, down a dirt road. The turn was so sudden that Will barely stayed upright. Luckily, the two giant wolves tripped over one another and crashed into a parked car. But they quickly scrambled and were up again.

The trio followed the eagle downhill, gravity boosting their speed. The eagle flew back between the bikes and called, *"Up ahead, not a peep, you'll have to take a faithful leap. Hurry now, you will see, climb the rope into the tree."*

Sure enough, at the end of the beaten path was the largest tree Will had ever seen. Near the top of the tulip poplar was a wooden tree house. A thick rope hung down from it.

"Don't bother to brake," Ivy shouted, "Aim your bikes for the ropes. Then make like Tarzan and jump!"

"We cannot do that!" Linus shouted back.

"Yes, we can!" Ivy shouted. "Count of three. One—two—*three*!!"

All three leaped off their bikes, flew through the air, and grabbed the rope. Ivy scurried up the rope as fast as a squirrel. Will was just behind her. But Linus wasn't nearly as strong or agile as his friends, and his massive backpack weighed him down. He barely made it up a few feet when he slipped. The first of the werewolves arrived, stretching up and grabbing his pants in its mouth.

"Help!" Linus cried out, barely clinging to the rope.

"Linus!" Ivy screamed. She was already rushing back down the rope. But Will was closer.

He dropped down, kicking the wolf in the face. Then he pushed his friend up, out of the wolf's reach. Ivy helped Linus, and Will clambered up from behind. Only the second werewolf jumped up, chomping at Will's ankle. Will cried out, kicking at the massive beast. From above, Ivy and Linus grabbed hold of the line and pulled as hard as they could, carrying Will up.

Both wolves vaulted and howled and chomped at the tree trunk below. But neither beast was coordinated enough to climb up after its prey.

As Will reached the top, Ivy and Linus dragged him up and over, into the old tree house. Exhausted, the three collapsed into a giant pile, hugging each other and shouting cheers of joy.

"Woo! We did it!" Ivy cried out. "What a rush!"

"Is everyone okay?" Linus asked, his heart pounding.

"Heck yeah! Let's do that again!" Ivy said. "What's more awesome than surviving a werewolf chase without a scratch?"

Will's face grew pale. "About that…"

Linus and Ivy turned. Will's pant leg was ripped open, and shining red dripped down from a large bite.

Dearest Reader, do not be upset. This should hardly be a surprise. After all, this is how the chapter began. And again, Will was not dead—it just *felt* like his life was over. And that feeling threatened to overwhelm him. Anyways…

The full moon shone through the tree house window, the light falling on Will. Thick hair began to overtake his legs, his hands, his arms, and soon, his face. His teeth began to grow, his eyes changing to black. He gazed up at the large circle of light in the night sky and howled.

Then he looked at Ivy and Linus, and his mouth began to water…

Chapter 2
Magic Among the Trees

✳

The sun had barely risen over the most eastern tip of Massachusetts when Will woke. He was lying in the tree house, curled into a ball, his tail tickling his face.

"Tail?!" Will sat up, shaking his head.

He looked down at his body. He was as hairy as a dog. Or worse—a wolf! He recalled last night, being bitten by a werewolf, then changing, then looking at his two best friends like they might make a satisfying squirrel supper...

He couldn't remember if he had—*gulp*—eaten them.

Will surveyed the tree house. They were nowhere to be seen. Will feared the worst. He shouted, "Ivy!? Linus?! Please don't be dead!"

"Dead?" Ivy yawned from above. She and Linus were twenty feet higher, tied to a large tree branch. "Takes a lot more than a werewolf to kill us."

"Did I—?" Will started to ask, not wanting to know the answer.

"You tried to masticate us, but we were far faster," Linus noted. "We ascended up here, out of your reach."

"Wait—have we been sleeping here all night?" Will asked, his heart stopping. Something much worse occurred to him than being bitten by a wolf—his mom finding out he hadn't come home last night. "Why did you let me fall asleep?!"

"Um, seriously?" Ivy asked. "You were a werewolf. And you were being all…wolfy. We didn't want to get bit."

"We have to get home," Will said. He leaped over the side of the tree house and started climbing down the rope. Ivy and Linus scrambled down after him. At the base of the tree, they found Will's and Linus's bikes. They mounted them and started pedaling home.

"It is still early," Linus said. "If we hurry, and sneak in, our parents might never know we were gone."

💀💀💀

Mom's car was in the driveway. He wondered if she'd been up all night worried sick. If she had been, he was dead. She would probably kill him.

Dear Reader, when Will believes his mom would kill him,

he truly believes she would murder him. Not out of anger, mind you, but out of love. I am told that (human) parents get truly upset when they cannot find their offspring. It is difficult for me to comprehend, probably because my parents wanted to be rid of me as soon as I was born.

So Will very carefully stepped up one porch step and then the other. Then he tiptoed over and opened the front door slowly…until it creaked. It was so loud, it might as well have screamed. Will panicked and rushed inside. He raced up the stairs, past his mom's closed door, ran into his room, and hopped into his own bed.

Usually, Fitz would have been glad to see him. But Fitz wasn't used to a werewolf version of Will. Sensing this was all wrong, Fitz leaped up and started barking.

Will barked back.

Fitz backed away, confused. Will threw his hands over his mouth, remembering that he was still a werewolf. He dove under his sheets.

"Are you up, mijo?" his mom called. She opened his door.

"Oh, um… I just woke up," Will said from beneath the blanket.

"I fell asleep early last night. I didn't even hear you come in from your friend's house," Mom noted. "Um, Guillermo, why are you hiding under there?"

"I'm…cold?" was what Will said. But only because he didn't want his mom to see his transformation. He was covered in hair. There was no way the town curse could hide that—could it?

For a moment, his thoughts raced: What was Mom going to do when she saw Will was a werewolf? Would she lose her mind? Would she ground him? Would she send him to the pound? Would she lock him onto an operating table within a metal cage to be raised to the top of a tower during a lightning storm?

Oh, wait, that was what my father did to me. Never mind.

"Can I please see your face?" Mom asked.

"It's the same face you see every day," Will lied.

"Guillermo, por favor," Ms. Vásquez said.

"I can't!" Will said.

"Will, you know I don't like secrets. Now take off those covers so I can see you, right this minute!"

Dearest Reader—as I'm sure you know—all children keep secrets from their parents. I, your humble author, neither advise nor condemn this practice. In fact, I appreciate its necessity. Though I would like to impart a bit of wisdom. As a Buddhist monk in Bangladesh once told me, *Three things cannot be long hidden: the sun, the moon, and the truth.* Which means the truth will always come out.

So Will decided to face the music sooner rather than later. He took a deep, shaky breath, then pulled the comforter back. Mom raised an eyebrow at him. "See? Was that so hard?"

"You don't…see anything different about me?" Will asked.

Luckily for Will, the town curse did its job. It did not allow anyone to see the magical, monstrous truths of the town—except those who are magical or monstrous themselves. So, when Ms. Vásquez looked at her son, she saw only her son—and *not* a hair-covered, potentially flea-ridden wolf-boy.

Mom took a closer look at her son. "Should I? Is this a puberty thing?"

"Ew, Mom. Never mind," Will said, pulling the blanket back over his head.

Ms. Vásquez patted her son's head. "Well, I got called in to the hospital early today. I need to head out. I know it's Saturday, but please do your homework before you go have fun. Hot dogs are in the fridge for lunch. Te amo siempre."

Will took a deep breath. He was relieved Mom couldn't see his change. He had to fix this. As soon as he heard Mom leave, he pulled the blanket from his head.

His dog growled, snarling his teeth.

"It's me, Fitz," Will said. He slowly reached out a hand for his dog to sniff. "It's me. I know, I'm a little different, but it's still me. I promise."

Fitz sniffed at him. The Saint Bernard walked slowly around Will, sniffing every inch of him. He spent an unusually long time sniffing Will's butt until Will shooed him away. "See? It's me." Fitz looked Will in the eye. Will smiled. "It's me, boy." Fitz gave Will's furry face a lick.

But instead of feeling relief, Will realized…he was a monster.

He picked up his walkie-talkie and radioed his friends. "You guys there?" He looked outside his window.

On the opposite side of the street, Ivy appeared in her bedroom window wearing a pajama set dotted with soccer balls. She spoke into her walkie-talkie. "Why does it have it to be *you guys*? Why not *you girls*? Why does society allow people to assume that if there's one boy and one girl, the language has to be rounded over to the male gender?"

"I'll take that as a yes," Will said, giving a wave. "Did you two make it in okay?"

"Yup. Parents were still asleep when we got in," Ivy said.

"Glad to hear," Will said.

"Everything okay? Did your mom notice you…you know…got a little wolfy?"

"Nope. Thank goodness for the town curse. But I'm totally freaking out," Will admitted, looking at one of his hands. It was almost as hairy as Fitz's paw, and his nails had grown longer and thicker, just like his teeth. "It's one thing to see a nice werewolf teaching math. It's completely different to become a late-night snack for shape-shifting wolves. Am I going to be stuck like this forever? Is there a cure? What if I hurt somebody? What if I start howling at the moon? What do I tell my dad—"

"Buy a flea collar?" Ivy asked.

"Har-har," Will said. "Ivy, I'm serious. I'm a werewolf. This is not what I signed up for. Is it hot? I'm hot. I can't breathe."

"Be careful, you'll have an anxiety attack. Take some

deep breaths and come over," Ivy said. "We'll put our heads together and figure it out."

"Fine," Will said, "I'll be there soon."

Will intended to take a quick shower, but soon realized it took a lot longer to wash a body covered completely in fur. He wasn't sure whether he should use soap or shampoo. He figured if he had to be a giant furball, he might as well have a silky coat. So after shampooing all over, he used conditioner. It took forever to rinse off.

Stepping onto the bath mat, he instinctively shook—like Fitz always did when he was wet—spraying water all over the bathroom. "Use a towel, dummy," he reminded himself. "You're still at least half human." He wiped steam from the mirror and almost screamed at his reflection. His face was covered in fur, his eyes seemed bigger, and his ears ended in little tufts of hair. What was he going to do? He couldn't live like this. Didn't dogs age faster than people? He'd be an old man before he was finished with high school. He tried to stay calm, but it wasn't working.

He put on a different pair of jeans and grabbed a shirt from his messy floor. The shirt smelled. He grabbed another one under a pile of *MonsterWorld* comics. This one didn't smell as bad. He wondered if he should get a jacket.

Then he remembered he already had a fur coat. He was so upset, his hands wouldn't stop shaking.

Across the street, he knocked on the Crosses' front door. For a second, he got freaked out that Mr. Cross would freak out when he saw Will's new furry face.

But thanks to the town curse, Mr. Cross smiled happily and said, "Good morning, Will. Ivy said you were coming over. You must be a good influence. Usually Ivy doesn't wake up on Saturdays before noon."

"I like sleeping in too," Will admitted sheepishly, trying to steady his hands. "Mom calls me huesos perezosos."

Mr. Cross laughed. "Lazy bones. I like that."

Will was surprised. "You speak Spanish?"

"Solo un poco. I took Español in college." Mr. Cross smiled. "Speaking of, how is your mom? No damage to your house or car I hope?"

"What do you mean?"

"Didn't you hear about last night? A pack of wolves tore through town. Trashed two neighborhoods. A few people were even bitten. Luckily, no one was seriously injured." Mr. Cross handed Will the town newspaper, the *East Emerson Exposé*. The front page's headline said:

Wild Animals Attack Town!

Local officials baffled by bizarre animal behavior.

"Kinda scary, right? I just got off the phone with a friend who was nearly attacked outside a grocery store. Almost gave her a heart attack. Luckily, she made it to her car in time before the critter got her. It threw itself at the window a few times before it got distracted by a cat."

"Was she bit?!" Will asked.

"No. But please, be careful out there. I already warned my kids, but they ignored me—as usual. I'm really glad you three started going to and from school together. Keep an eye on them, will you?" Mr. Cross headed toward the kitchen. "Have you had breakfast? I was about to make omelets and fresh bambalouni, which are basically donuts."

Will's stomach grumbled. He felt his face flush as he thought of the hot dogs for lunch—again. "Oh, um, it's okay. I have food at home."

"Nonsense. Breakfast is the most important meal of the day, you know. I was about to cook for the kids anyway. You might as well join us. Go ahead upstairs. I'll let you know when it's ready." Mr. Cross disappeared into the kitchen.

Will couldn't hide his smile. His dad used to make him breakfast too. Pancakes, hash browns, French toast, scrambled eggs, bacon—extra crispy, just the way he liked it. Will tried not to wonder if his dad would ever cook for him again. But when he remembered he was a werewolf, the shaking panic returned.

Upstairs, Will found Ivy at a door. She jiggled the doorknob, glancing at Will before turning her attention back to her work. "See? It's locked. But watch this…" Ivy pulled a small case from her pocket. Inside were several skinny metal tools. Ivy chose two of them, placed them into the door's lock, moved them around, and the door opened.

"How did you—?"

Ivy grinned. "My parents kept locking up my skateboard for bad behavior. So I learned how to pick locks online. Cool, huh, Will… Or should I call you *wolf-man*?"

"Come on," Will said, covering his face. "I'm already insecure enough."

"You shouldn't be. You're as cute as a *puppy*!" Ivy laughed.

Linus appeared at the door across the hall. He rolled his eyes. "Please ignore my sister."

Will turned to his other friend. "Can you see me?"

"Of course I can see you."

"I mean, can you see that I'm a werewolf?"

Linus shook his head. "I observe nothing but your normal visage."

"Town curse," Ivy noted.

Will entered and paced Linus's room, staring at his shaking furry hands. "I'm a freak. A monster! A werewolf! What am I going to do? Is there a cure? What if I'm stuck like this forever? Do I have to start eating dog food? By the way, your dad is really cool. He's making us breakfast."

Ivy shrugged. "Who cares about breakfast? You're a werewolf."

"I know!" Will answered. He felt hysterical panic rise up his throat as he kept pacing. He felt like if he stopped walking, he would scream.

"Cause chaos. Bite people. Pee on fire hydrants," Ivy said.

"As always, my sister is the opposite of helpful." Linus turned to his computer and typed *werewolf* into a search engine.

Will tried to think. "Well, in my *MonsterWorld* comics, werewolves can't control themselves. Around the full moon, they are totally taken over by their instincts. Sometimes the moon's effects last the night before and the night after too."

Linus typed on his keyboard. He turned the monitor to his friends. "Or perhaps you are wrong. Given the unlikelihood of being infected by a strain of lycanthropy, I believe a much more likely diagnosis for the Neighborhood Watch and yourself is this: a case of hypertrichosis, a rare condition characterized by excessive growth of hair in abnormal places. Someone dubbed it *werewolf syndrome* due to the similarities."

"If that were the case, you would be able to see the hair on Will's face," Ivy said. "Since you can't, the problem is magical."

"Or perhaps you and Will are pranking me," Linus stated.

"When do I ever prank you?" Ivy asked defensively.

"All of the time." Linus pointed up. "Exhibit A: you stapled all of my clean underwear to the ceiling."

"That wasn't me," Ivy said. "Those are the *Flelfs*."

"Flelfs do not exist."

"If East Emerson has taught me anything, it's this: any supernatural creature you think exists, *does*." Will put his hand on Linus's shoulder and looked him in the eye. "Linus, I'm not lying. This is not a trick. I'm a werewolf."

Linus examined the fear in Will's eyes. He breathed out a heavy sigh. "I suppose I believe you...but I feel terrible. You saved me last night from those wild dogs—"

"They were werewolves!" Ivy corrected.

"My point being," Linus said, "Will saved me and now he needs help."

"What he needs is a cool haircut. Have you seen those poodles with dyed pink hair and their backs shaved into Mohawks?"

"As always, my sister's capacity for compassion and emotional support is found lacking," Linus stated. "We need to help our friend. What are we going to do?"

"Let's go to the pet store and get Will a leash," Ivy said. "I'll take you on walks—but I am *not* picking up your poop."

Will growled at his friend—but like, actually *growled*, like a wolf. That is, like a *were*wolf. He grabbed his mouth in horror. "Sorry! I can't help it!"

"Enough jokes, Ivy," Linus said. "Will needs help. Which means we need to go see the expert on all things magical in this town—the witch in the woods."

💀💀💀

"Yikes," Ivy said. "Check it out. The town is totally trashed."

Riding their bikes, the three friends surveyed the damage in the nearby neighborhoods. It looked as though East

Emerson had had a massive party that got out of hand. Trash cans were overturned, mailboxes were knocked off their posts, store windows were broken, and signs were lying facedown in the streets, like they were dead.

"It's like the newspaper said," Will whispered, "but why would werewolves do this?"

"I don't know, but looks like the locals aren't happy about it." Ivy nodded to those collected on the sidewalks. "The supernatural folks look just as annoyed as the regular people."

Two reanimated revenants walked down the streets, holding hands, moaning about the mess. Weasel-like ramidreju snuck out of the woods to sniff for gold, only to find fur and blood. A reptilian-humanoid family came outside and found their car turned upside down. And three neighbors—an eight-foot-tall robot, a ten-foot-tall rephaite, and a roku-rokubi whose neck was almost twelve feet long—gathered to complain about their lawns being turned into litter boxes.

Will had only lived in East Emerson for a month, and already he knew this town was full of impossible creatures. Still, he couldn't help but gasp anytime he saw some supernatural being. Beloved Reader, do not think Will a fraidy-cat. If you saw living machines and ancient giants and long-necked spirits that no one else could see, you'd probably walk around gasping too.

The three friends turned off a paved road and onto a dirt path. Riding west, they passed the well where they first met Oracle Jones and her lemur, Gumbo. Will needed to remember to ask Oracle about the mysterious gray stranger, the one who had saved Will, Ivy, and Linus, not just from giant spiders, but from Ozzie herself—even as the stranger had revealed that he worked for the wicked witch. Will wondered if they would see him again. Something in his gut said yes. But would the stranger be a friend or a foe next time?

After locking their bikes together against a fence, Will and Ivy noticed a handmade sign that said:

wlm'g gzpv zmlgsvi hgvk.
Gszg'h irtsg, R szev blfi "hvxivg" xlwv, 13.
zmw nb slnv rh kilgvxgvw yb nztrx uiln
gsv orpvh lu blf.
Gzpv zmlgsvi hgvk, zmw nvvg blfi nzpvi,
'xfa nb hkvooh droo proo blf wvzw.
—L

"Rad," Ivy said. "Oracle knows the code the Thirteen are using."

"She seems to know everything," Will noted.

"Probably because she's psychic," Ivy said.

The trio searched out the two giant trees that marked the entrance to Oracle Jones's property. Strange symbols were carved into both trunks, which glowed as they passed between them. Another tree had odd words carved into its trunk that read:

Tutum Domus

"Another code?" Will asked.

"Nah, just Latin," Ivy said. Linus and Will stared at her. "What? You two can't read Latin?"

Will shook his head. "Uh, no. You can?"

Ivy shrugged, then walked ahead. "I'm good with languages."

As they passed under a set of weeping willows, a swarm of tiny pests stormed around them. "Infernal creatures!" Linus said, swatting at them.

But Will grabbed his hands. "Stop! Don't kill any! Those are sprites, remember?!"

Ivy squinted. Sure enough, the mosquitoes were being ridden by tiny men in little saddles. "I wonder if these guys could help me cheat on tests. They could whisper the answers in my ear."

"Or you could try studying," Linus said.

"That's not nearly as fun," Ivy said.

The three followed the path of doll heads propped up on sticks. As they passed, the plastic faces turned, all at once, to watch them. A breeze blew, and the sound of clacking clucked through the air from the hundreds of bones tied to the trees like wind chimes. Ivy asked, "Do you think those are human bones?"

Linus winced. He squinted through his glasses. "No, those are the bones of animals. Judging by size and shape, I would conjecture those are the remains of birds, pigs, and horses."

"Cool," Ivy said.

"Creepy," Will said.

"I got ya, ya danged critter! Ain't no escapin' Oracle Jones!" The witch's voice came from somewhere deep within the thick, overgrown garden. The three friends followed the sound of her grunts and heaves until they saw the wild nest of fire-red hair jerking back and forth. Her cowboy boots kept her planted while she wrenched her entire body right and left as she yanked on deer antlers lodged in a nearby bush. The sleeveless button-up cowboy shirt had silver thread worked into the plaid lines that shimmered under the sun finding its way through the green canopy overhead.

Oracle Jones gave another yank and ripped a strange beast from the brambles. It was a large rabbit with antlers coming out of its forehead. "Caught ya, ya troublemaker. Now you listen here. Next time I catch ya eatin' plants in my herb garden, I'll be eatin' *jackalope* stew for dinner. Ya got me?"

Linus shook his head. "Jackalopes do not exist."

"Says you," Oracle laughed, holding up her catch.

"You know I cannot see magical creatures," Linus said. "All I see is a jackrabbit."

"A rabbit with horns," Will said.

Linus stomped his foot on the ground, frustrated. "I am part and parcel of our Supernatural Society! I deserve to see magic things with my own eyes too, don't I?!"

The blind witch shook her head no. "Is that what y'all came for?"

"No," Will said, pointing his claws at his face. "I kinda got bit last night."

"Hrmph," Oracle grunted. "In my vision, I coulda sworn it'd be the boy with glasses who'da gotten bit."

"It was supposed to be," Linus said. "But Will saved me."

Oracle took a step toward Will, as if she could see him through the bandanna tied over her eyes. "You changed fate. Fas-cin-atin'."

"Wait," Linus asked, "if Will bites me, will I be able to see magic then?"

"Nah," Oracle answered. "No magic sight for lycans— not unless you're an Alpha or a natural-born shape-shifter. A typical werewolf is still mostly human, and Emerson's town curse keeps 'em in the dark as much as regular folk. They won't even recall what they done did as wolves. But come on now. No time for dawdlin'." Oracle wiped her freckled brow and waved for the others to follow. "Y'all are late. We was expectin' y'all tomorrow."

"If you were expecting us *tomorrow*, then we're *early*," Linus noted.

"Don't go startin' with that logic nonsense. If you saw past, present, and future all at once, time'd get mighty confusin' for you too." The wrinkled old witch stepped behind one tree and instantly appeared behind another nearly a hundred feet away. "Now let's go."

The jackalope struggled to escape from Oracle Jones without success. Despite her age and frail form, the woman was far from fragile. She walked effortlessly around trees, ducking under branches and stepping over thorny black-rose bushes as though she could see them.

She led Will and the others around the side of her house, into her backyard. Massive white pines crawled up toward the sun, covering the backyard in so much shade that it began to feel like dusk. Oracle blew on a large red candle that had been melted onto a tree trunk. Its dead wick sparked to life, lighting itself with a tiny flame. Instantly, hundreds of other candles around the clearing lit themselves too. Oracle said, "Don't step on no graves."

Eerie candlelight illuminated the shadows, revealing hand-carved tombstones half hidden by black roses, thistles, and thorns. One said, "Here lies Jambalaya, killed by a griffin." Another read, "Rest in Peace, Po'Boy." Others included:

"In memory of my little Muffuletta,"

"You were too good for this earth, Cajun Rémoulade,"

"Always in my cold dead heart, Rice & Beans,"
"Faithful and never forgotten, Fried Chicken,"
"Sleep easy, Andouille," and "1910–1918, My girl, Grits."

"What new ridiculousness is this?" Linus asked. "Are you burying your meals out here?"

Faster than a snake, Oracle leaped over and grabbed Linus's tongue. "Watch that mouth. I don't mind you dis-respectin' *me*, but I won't have ya talkin' ill of the *dead*—'specially not any of my past familiars."

"Familiars?" Will asked. "As in witches' pets?"

Oracle flashed a white smile, the red freckles on her skin almost glowing in the candlelight. "Familiars are more than pets. They're companions, friends, personal assistants, and cuter than a button. Muffuletta was a Scottish fold cat. Rice and Beans were racoons. And Fried Chicken was an Austra-lian cattle dog. Saved my life more than once. Fought off a Syrian Sphinx while I was dyin' of a cobra bite. Any of you would be lucky to have a friend like that."

Will thought of his own dog. Last month, Fitz was turned into a vampire but never stopped protecting him.

Luckily, Fitz wasn't a vampire anymore, which gave Will some hope that he too might one day be normal again... Either way, when he got home, Will would make sure to give Fitz an extra-big hug. But for now, he needed help. "Werewolves ran wild last night. We think there's a new big bad on the island."

The old woman cackled. "Ain't nothin' new. Just old stuff comin' back to haunt us in the present. Ozzie's got one of her Thirteen turning folks into lycans. They go tearing up the town 'cause they can't control themselves. Will would be joining 'em tonight if not for me. Why ya think ol' Gumbo and I be workin' all mornin' to prep a witch's brew for the boy?" Oracle waved her hand and a curtain of vines and tree limbs and leaves moved aside. Behind it, a dark tunnel of vegetation led farther into the shadows of the thick forest.

Will and Ivy followed. Linus, on the other hand, crossed his arms defensively and mumbled under his breath, "...dumb old witch, putting her dirty hand in my mouth, tasted like turpentine, one of these days I'm gonna prove all her magic is just ludicrous nonsense..." Linus kicked the nearest tree.

The tree moaned, *"Ow! Don't do that."* But due to the town curse, Linus didn't hear it.

In the center of a dark clearing, a small fire blazed beneath a black cauldron. The green bubbling stew was being stirred by Gumbo Jones, Oracle's ring-tailed lemur. The animal familiar screeched in response to their arrival.

"Hush now, little man," Oracle said. "I know ya missed lunchtime. But work comes first." The primate shrieked again. This time the witch glared at him. "Don't yell at me! I'm not a nitwit—I have the last ingredient right here!" She held the jackalope up by its antlers.

The old witch placed the jackalope on a stone slab and raised a large metallic axe into the air. Will, Ivy, and Linus closed their eyes.

Thunk!

Will forced himself to look. He sighed a breath of relief. Oracle hadn't killed the creature—she'd merely cut off the tip of its antler. She tossed it into the stew. "Don't worry none, it'll grow back," Oracle said. Then to the jackalope said, "Thank ya for your contribution. Now off with ya. And stay outta my herb garden!" Once she let go, the horned rabbit scurried away in a flash to find its burrow. "Now, where was we?"

"We need your help with the werewolves," Ivy said.

"We saw one of Ozzie's codes painted on a fence, but we could not decipher it with the golden pyramid," Linus continued. "But it certainly means she is involved again."

"And, uh, it'd be great if you could fix me," Will finished.

Oracle sniffed at Will. "You was bit last night. Not by an Alpha, but by...a freshly turned Omega."

"Explain," Linus said.

Oracle stirred the cauldron. "Werewolves are like any other pack of dogs. They organize socially for huntin' and maintainin' stability in the group. There's always an Alpha, a pack leader—that's the one in charge. Then there's a Beta, the second-in-command. Then there's the rest, Gammas, Deltas, et cetera, all of which take orders. On the lowest rung are the Omegas, usually the newest turned, also the weakest. The others'll bully him or her, to remind 'em of the pecking order."

"Sounds like middle school," Ivy said.

"Yes, thank you for the wildlife lesson," Linus scoffed. "Any child knows this from watching Nat Geo. Can you get on with giving Will the cure for lycanthropy?"

Oracle Jones laughed so hard she started coughing. She hacked up a huge ball of phlegm and spit it into the boiling cauldron. "There *ain't* a cure—unless you're talking about a silver bullet through the heart."

Will's face turned pale. "Are you serious?"

"As a heart attack," the witch said.

Will felt like gravity was suddenly stronger. Like his heart weighed a ton and was falling into his stomach. No cure?

"Sorry, boy. Some things done cannot be undone. As with science, there are rules in magic—that includes shape-shifters…"

"Can you tell us the rules?" Linus asked, pulling out a pad of paper and a pen, ready to take notes.

"*Rule #1:* Werewolves are normal folk who turn into wolves. They only turn full wolf on a full moon. The rest of the month, they're stuck somewhere between. Some look human, others look like Will. Fur-faced and waggin' tail. Here in East Emerson, the town curse keeps people from even knowing what they are…

"That said, Alphas can turn into wolves whenever they want. Especially if ya make them mad. But moving on.

"*Rule #2:* Once bitten, a werewolf is sired to the pack. Any member of the pack *must* do what the Alpha tells 'em to, whether in wolf or human form. Essentially, they can't say no to the Alpha's mental commands.

"*Rule #3:* Werewolves are stronger, faster, and tougher than humans. Have heightened senses too, especially smell. They also heal a whole lot faster.

"*Rule #4:* A werewolf can only be killed in three ways—ingestin' wolfsbane, silver through the heart, or cuttin' off their head."

Ivy patted Will's back. "Jeez, that's rough. Sorry, bud."

"Are you absolutely certain that there is no cure?" Linus asked. "Perhaps a medication? A once-a-month pill?"

Oracle shook her head. "Not that I heard of. Though I admit, I know a lot, but not everything…"

Will sank to the ground like a deflated balloon. "So I'll turn into an animal once a month? That's not good. What if the Alpha makes me stay out all night? Or rob banks? My mom'll flip out. What am I supposed to do?"

"You could always *become* the pack leader," Ivy said. "I mean, if I was gonna be a weregirl, I'd at least wanna be in charge."

Will looked hopeful. He turned his face to Oracle. "How do I become the Alpha?"

Oracle Jones stuck her finger into the boiling cauldron and tasted it. "Easy. *Rule #5:* Become the new Alpha by killing the old Alpha."

"I can't kill someone!" Will squeaked. "There's gotta be a different way."

Oracle Jones plucked a coffee mug from a nearby tree branch. She ladled the boiling green ooze into it and handed it to Will. "Well, this'll help."

"What is it?"

"It'll protect ya from heartworm, fleas, and ticks, and give you a shiny coat."

"Yeah, no. I am not drinking that," Will said.

"It'll take away your wolf powers for the most part, but also help ya refuse the commands of the Alpha—at least until the next full moon."

"What happens on the full moon?"

The witch gritted her teeth. "You become full wolf and do whatever the Alpha tells ya. My advice? Find some chains and lock yourself up in a basement far from anyone else. You'll hear the commands in your mind, but if you're tied up nice and tight, won't be able to execute 'em—or any*one*."

Begrudgingly, Will took the mug. The steaming sludge looked like vomit.

Usually Ivy would take this opportunity to make a joke. But she felt truly bad for Will, especially after he saved her brother. So instead, she squeezed his shoulder and nod-ded. "Drink it, Will. If it helps, it helps."

Will closed his eyes and downed the drink in one gulp. When he was done, he yelled, *"THAT WAS TOO HOT!"*

Oracle shook her head. "Ya could have waited till it cooled down, dummy."

The old witch filled two large terra-cotta jugs with the green sludge. When they were full, she corked them and handed them to Will. "Drink half a cup twice each day—when you wake and before you sleep. You'll still be a bit wolfy round the edges, but you won't have to obey no commands—verbal or telepathic."

"Tele-what?" Ivy asked.

"Telepathy. It's when you can read or control thoughts," Will said.

"You read too many *MonsterWorld* comics," Ivy noted.

Will shrugged. "Seems to come in handy, though, doesn't it?" He nodded to the jugs of muck and thanked Oracle.

Linus was counting on his fingers. "Last night was the full moon. That means we have twenty-eight and a half days to stop Will from becoming a wolf. How shall we start?"

Ivy pulled out the black tourmaline necklaces she wore around her neck. She flashed them at the witch. "You gave us these last time, and they stopped mind control. Can you give us anything to protect against werewolves?"

"I got this." Oracle tossed a bag full of onions to Linus and Ivy. "Don't wanna get bit? Rub yourself with white onions. It'll make your eyes tear up mighty fierce, but wolves'll hate ya. They hate onions, smells like wolfsbane—which works best, but mighty hard to find."

"Thanks," Will said. "Anything else you can tell us? Why Ozzie wants werewolves? What the silver fox wants us to do? What we should do next?"

The lemur hopped onto Oracle's shoulder and screeched at Will. Oracle shook her head in agreement. "You said it, Gumbo. Boy asks too many questions."

"You have to give us something more."

"I don't *have* to do nothin'," Oracle yelled. "Truth be told, I don't want no part of this battle 'tween good and evil. I done lost too much to this war already!"

The kids had never seen Oracle upset. But Gumbo pet her face, kissed her cheek, then chattered something into her ear. The witch calmed down. "Ignore my outburst. I just… I wish this path you're on was gonna be easy, but it ain't. You're gonna lose things ya treasure along the way. That's what happens in war. Sacrifices must be made."

"Sacrifices?" Will whispered. He wondered if this meant he was stuck as a werewolf.

"You see the future, right?" Ivy asked. "Isn't there anything you can tell us?"

"I wish I could. But sometimes the truth is dangerous—'specially if you learn it too early."

Flustered, Will asked, "Can't you help us fight the werewolves? Or maybe help me become the Alpha so I can take charge and stop them from wrecking the town?"

Oracle turned her back. "No."

"*Those who choose to sit on the side and wait are often forgotten when it comes to fate,*" said a voice from above. The silver fox was sitting on a branch in a tree nearby, glowing brightly. "*In the eternal battle for death and life, you must choose a side to battle the strife.*"

"Dina Iris Grave, you can go on and get outta here," Oracle snapped. "I did my part."

"*Dina Iris Grave,*" Will whispered. He couldn't explain how, but the magic fox's name seemed so obvious now, like he'd always known it.

"Who? What do you see?" Linus asked.

"The silver fox is here," Ivy whispered.

Dina Iris jumped down from the branch, but before her paws touched ground, she turned into a hummingbird and flew over to Oracle. *"No one promised life would be breezy. Nothing in life is ever easy."*

"I know that better than most, fox." The witch sat down on a tree trunk, glaring at the glowing hummingbird. Gumbo swatted the bird away, then petted Oracle's red hair gently, cooing in her ear. "I can't do anymore."

"One can always do more," Dina Iris whispered.

Oracle stood, shouting at the bird, "Ain't I done enough? I been helpin' ya for how long?! Reinforcin' ancient spells, callin' corners to keep storms at bay, brokerin' real estate deals—"

A chill ran up Will's spine. He didn't know why. What did real estate have to do with anything?

The witch continued to seethe, "—I done been helpin' ya for decades! A century now! I done plenty for ya and this accursed town! Ya know what I've lost. All it's gotten me is scars and a broken heart… Can't ya just let me be?" Tears trickled down from behind the bandanna covering the witch's eyes.

The glowing bird transformed into a radiant frog and leaped across the ground before shifting into a squirrel.

The puffy-tailed creature looked up at Will, Ivy, and Linus. *"You don't need an army to fight a war; three is enough to open any door. All you need is to have hope in your heart, and the battle is won before the start."*

"Yeah, I don't know," Ivy said, "I feel like hope is a good starting point, but a tank would be a whole lot more helpful. Got one of those?"

The squirrel ran up Linus's side onto his shoulder. She tapped on Linus's glasses. *"No——but a gift from a magical hag can offer up vision to eyes that lag."* The squirrel shifted back into the silver fox and landed next to Oracle's feet. *"One last favor..."*

"Oracle, please," Ivy said. "If my brother could just see what we see…"

The witch wiped her cheeks with the backs of her dirty hands. She glanced from Will to Ivy to Linus.

"Fine. I do this, and y'all best leave me alone. I done fought enough wolves to last ten fairy tales." Oracle stood up, walked over to Linus, and pulled the glasses off his face. She pulled a small primitive blade from her robe. With it, she began carving tiny symbols into the frames of Linus's glasses.

When she was done, she flipped the dagger around her

finger, offering the handle to Ivy. "It's an athame, made of pure silver. It ain't a gift. It's a borrow. Ya can return it when you're done. You'll know when to use it."

"Do I get a gift?" Will asked.

The old witch scowled. "Yeah, some advice: shut your mouth while I'm working."

"*Oracle, please,*" Dina Iris said. "*Do not tease.*"

The old witch took a deep, rough breath. "Fine. That gold pyramid in your pocket? Keep it with ya. It's how Ozzie talks to her Thirteen."

"We know." Will pulled the key stone from his pocket. "Dr. Pamiver told us as much before Ozzie killed him. Did you know the Thirteen are trying to dig up someone named Simon—"

Oracle Jones screamed. A burst of magic exploded from her, the energy shattering the cauldron and knocking Will, Ivy, and Linus to the ground. Oracle wheezed, pulling the bandanna from her face, revealing scarred eyeless sockets. "That…that…*warlock* is the truest monster I've ever met. Massacred hundreds of innocent souls, slaughtered them for his own personal gain. He is pure evil. Last time, it took everything we had to put him in the ground. Seven soldiers of fate, destined to die. Three of us survived, and just barely…" Oracle's voice trailed off as her face darkened. "*NEVER* speak his name in my presence again."

"I'm… I'm sorry," Will whispered. "I… I didn't know."

Ivy stepped forward. "What are you not telling us? Shouldn't we know everything before we fight for you?"

The witch turned her glare on the fox. "Ya better tell them to back off, or I *will* tell them the truth—the *whole* truth."

Dina Iris shook her head at Ivy. "*Some truths must wait. That is your fate.*"

Oracle Jones returned her attention to Linus's glasses. She held them to her heart, chanting, "*Videre verum. Videre verum. Videre verum.*" The glasses began to glow for a moment. Finally, Oracle stuck out her tongue and licked both lenses. She handed them back to Linus.

"You licked my glasses," Linus said.

"Put them on," Oracle snapped.

Linus did, and his eyes went wide. "*I… I can see.*"

"Of course you can see," Ivy said.

"No, I mean, I can see the real world—" Linus started, staring at Will's fur-covered face and hands and wagging tail. A mosquito landed on Linus's hand, and he saw a tiny sprite step down from his saddle and wave. Then Linus locked eyes with Dina Iris for the first time. At any other time, he would have made note that she was an island fox, *Urocyon littoralis*. But right now, with the little fox shining like moonlight, he could focus on nothing other than her beauty. Everything around him was beautiful to Linus in a way he'd never known. Magic made the world…*shimmer* with life. "I perceive magic, the supernatural, as it really is. Is this how you two always see?"

Ivy said, "Yup," and rubbed Linus's back, not realizing how overjoyed she was to have a brother who could see her world now.

"Welcome to the weird world," Will said with a smile. Warmth flooded his body. He too realized how good it felt to not be alone.

If only, Sweet Reader, this moment could have lasted a little longer.

Instead, the fox's smile vanished, her eyes darkened, and she spoke to the three friends: *"With magic sight, your eyes are free; now be prepared, battle comes for thee. With fur and fangs comes your plight, but be prepared, for you must fight."*

Chapter 3
howls in the hallway

✳

Linus fell off his bike no less than ten times on the way home from the woods. Now that he could see the supernatural, everywhere he looked was something absolutely shocking. Unlike Will and Ivy, Linus was not used to seeing East Emerson full of monsters, magic, myths, and mad science.

Dear Reader, have you ever seen something so extraordinarily outside the norm that you felt faint, breathless, on the verge of tears (or screams), and like you might pee yourself, all at the exact same time? Well, that's how Linus felt finally seeing what Ivy had been seeing for quite some time.

He saw gremlins watering gardens, gargoyles working at garages, and golems greeting grandparents at the senior center. If that wasn't enough, Linus also witnessed a gytrash gambling with a gui po; a gulon growling at a gumiho; a grigori riding a griffin; a gnome grabbing at a glashtyn for its gingerbread; and a gandaberunda giving granola and gummy bears to a gagana, a girtablilu, a gjenganger, and a gegenes. Oh, and a gichi-anami'e-bizhiw galloped in front of Linus's bike.

Excuse me? Confused Reader, of course I'm *not* making up these creature names. They exist! Ask your mom or your teacher or your local lamia librarian. You could even use a laptop or smartphone or whatever newfangled computer doohickey allows for search engines and the internet and the World Wide Web. (It's not actually a spider's web, is it?)

You don't believe me? Fine. Explanations then:

A gytrash is a black dog that haunts lonely roads. A gui po is a ghost that manifests as an old woman. A gulon is an overly hungry hodgepodge of a dog, a cat, and a fox. A gumiho is a demon fox with nine magic tails. A grigori is a fallen angel, and a griffin is a lion with the head and wings of an eagle. A gnome is a dimunitive earth elemental, and a glashtyn is a malevolent water horse. A gandaberunda is a two-headed magical bird, and a gagana is a bird with an iron beak and copper claws, while a girtablilu is half human, half scorpion. A gjenganger is a spirit or undead body fresh from the grave, and a gegenees is a giant with six arms. Oh, and a gichi-anami'e-bizhiw? That's a bison-snake-bird-cougar hybrid water spirit, sometimes called an underwater panther.

You see, the world has a long history with monsters. Most of them have just been in hiding for the last century. Many of them came to East Emerson. I know you thought I was just being silly. But I'm not silly. I'm a monster.

Back to my original point… Seeing so much supernatural totally freaked out poor Linus, whose heart was beating so hard, he worried it might burst from his chest and race down the street screaming. Not that hearts can scream, but he still worried about it.

When the three friends got home, Linus threw down his bike and shouted, "I am having a psychotic break! Or a schizophrenic episode! Or a midlife crisis!"

"You're too young for that," Will said.

"My point is, my scientific brain cannot process all that I am seeing."

"At least you don't have permanent wolf face," Ivy said, nodding toward Will.

"Please don't say it's permanent," Will said. "I have to

focus on fixing this. I mean, I'm still me, right?" But only a second later, a squirrel ran across the road and up a nearby tree. Will, unable to control himself, ran after it and started barking. When he realized what he was doing, he stopped.

"Well, I do believe I have seen enough insanity for one day. I need to go lie down." Linus went inside his house and shut the door.

"Think he's going to be okay?" Will asked.

Ivy nodded. "Yeah, he's had to put up with me for years. A few monsters won't mess him up too much. I mean, you just got here last month, and you're well-adjusted already."

"I don't know if I'd say that," Will whispered, glancing down at his hands, which looked more like paws.

His transformation reminded him of the strange nightmares he'd been having since he moved to town. In one, he was being chased by a dark man all in black. Then there was the one where he was in a room with lots of people, but no one could see him, including his father. Another dream took place in the tunnels beneath East Emerson, with Will lost in a labyrinth. But the worst, the one he had most often, was of waking up in school *naked*.

Will shuddered at the thought. "Do you ever wonder

why it's up to the three of us to save this town? I mean, we're just kids."

Ivy shook her head. "I try not to think about things too hard. Gives me a headache. Plus, living here beats being in a boring town."

"Does it?" Will whispered. "I wouldn't mind a little bit of boring for a while. I hate having so many questions. Like, why can I see the supernatural without the help of a magic ring like you or bewitched glasses like Linus?"

"Maybe you were born wrong," Ivy joked.

Will didn't laugh. He sometimes wondered if he *was* born broken or damaged somehow. That'd explain why his dad wouldn't call him back, why his parents got a divorce, why his mom was so broke. Maybe Will was cursed.

A knot formed in Will's gut, making him feel sick. "I think I'm gonna go home and lie down too. Catch ya later."

Will didn't sleep. Instead, he lay in bed, staring at his ceiling. Fitz lay beside him, as if keeping guard. He heard the front door open and the jingle of Mom's keys going in the dish next to the door. The stairs creaked as she walked up and into his room.

Ms. Vásquez stood in her nursing scrubs and offered her son a sympathetic smile. "Rough day?"

"Oh, um…kinda I guess."

"Want to talk about it? Talking helps."

He didn't want to talk about it. But he knew Mom wouldn't leave until he did. "I just… Would you still love me if I weren't normal?"

Mom sat down beside Will. "Mijo, what are you trying to say?"

"I think… I think there's something…wrong with me."

"Will, why on earth would you think that?"

"Because it's true. I'm not like other kids. I mean, aside from Ivy and Linus, I don't have any friends. You only like me because you have to. And it's pretty obvious Dad doesn't care. He probably has a new family or a better life 'cause I'm not around."

"Whoa, whoa, whoa, take a deep breath," Ms. Vásquez said. "You're going down a shame spiral, Guillermo, and for what? You are being too hard on yourself. First, we only moved here a month ago. Having two friends is a great start. And I choose to love you, with all of my heart. I even like you, not because I have to, but because you're very likable. As for your father, if he isn't smart enough to call you back, it's his loss. You are wonderful, Will. You are brave and smart and handsome and—"

"You *have* to say all that stuff. You're my mom."

"Wrong. I don't have to say any of it. But I do say it, because it's true. Now come here." Mom wrapped her arms around Will, squeezing him tight. He wished it felt like it used to when he was little, when Mom and Dad would hug him at the same time. Between the two of them, he always felt warm and safe. But he didn't feel that now. He hadn't felt that in a long time.

💀💀💀

Will crossed the street with his bike. Ivy and Linus were waiting to ride to school together. Will asked, "How you feeling about everything?"

"Much better," Linus admitted. "My mind needed a few days to process how many varieties of supernatural creature East Emerson has to offer. Rather than let it consume me with abject terror, I have decided to approach it with eager enthusiasm, as Charles Darwin surely did while drafting *The Origin of Species*."

Ivy rolled her eyes. "Is that a science thing?"

"Science is cool," Linus stated with certainty.

Ivy pulled a foil ball from her backpack. She unwrapped

it, revealing an onion cut in two. She handed half to her brother.

"Do we have to?" Linus asked.

Ivy nodded. "If we don't want to get hairy, like Will here."

The two did as Oracle Jones instructed. They rubbed the onions on their necks, chest, wrists, forearms, and ankles. Their eyes were tearing up, even as Will stepped back, cupping his nose in his furry palms. "Well, that certainly works. My new wolf nose hates that smell. It's actually burning my brain, you stink so bad."

"Always nice to hear," Ivy said sarcastically. She tossed the onion to Will. "Want some?"

"Ew! No!" he said, tossing it from one hand to the other, then tossing it back.

Will made sure to ride at the front of the three bikes, upwind from the onion stench. When the three friends arrived at school, they split up to visit their lockers before class. Walking alone, Linus noticed that the hallways were filled with weird. One of his teachers was a robot. Another was a ghost. And he could have sworn he saw a classroom door shut and vanish, as if it melted into the bricks. But that was impossible, wasn't it?

Two students stood at a table with a large sign saying

CANNED FOOD DRIVE!

One of them called out to Linus, "Thanksgiving is coming, and what better way to give thanks than to give back?
Donate any canned goods?"

"I will make certain to bring some tomorrow," Linus said.
But as he walked on by, he noticed several strange blue-
skinned creatures sitting in the donation box, opening
the cans with their claws and pouring the contents into
their mouths, swallowing them whole. Linus took a deep
breath and kept walking, whispering to himself the advice his sister had given him: "Do not mess with them, and
they will not mess with me—"

Behind him, someone shouted, "Yo, Four Eyes—*catch*!"

POW! A football slammed into Linus's face, bounced off the
locker door, then hit him a second time. Linus tripped over
his own foot and crashed to the ground, spilling his books.

Giant football player Digby Bronson and his friends
laughed. "Nice catch…*loser.*"

Linus squeezed his fingers into fists. He wanted to
punch the jerk. Instead, he took a deep breath and reminded himself that logic and reason were far better

weapons. "Please move aside or I'll be forced to report you and your cohorts to the principal—"

SLAM!

Digby body slammed Linus into the lockers. He laughed again. "Oops. My bad. Guess I don't know my own strength. Catch ya later, pip-squeak."

Linus stayed on the ground until Digby began to walk away. He checked his glasses, thankful that they weren't broken, just as Ivy rounded the corner.

"Hey! What happened? Why are you on the ground?"

"Last month, I had a welcome break from bullies, because they were all too tired and bloodsucked to bother me. I help save the town from vampires, and my reward is a return to my usual daily routine here at school—being picked on and harassed." Linus sighed.

"Who was it?" Ivy asked, smacking her right fist into her left palm. "Give me names."

"Though I appreciate your enthusiasm, please do not attempt to fight my battles. That will only make things worse if it appears I cannot stand up for myself."

Ivy growled under her breath as Will approached.

"Everything okay?"

"My brother is being bullied," Ivy grunted.

"Want me to go bite someone?" Will joked.

"Um, you might be about to get bit yourself," Ivy said.

Gertrude York and Penelope Bosworth had appeared on either side of Will and started…well, *sniffing* him.

The two girls started at his neck, then went down to his armpits, and even his…*ahem*…butt. Unable to stop himself, Will found himself sniffing them back. The three were sniffing each other all over, their three tails wagging. Gertrude's and Penelope's faces were as furry as Will's.

Will blushed. "How are you ladies doing today?"

The girls stopped. Their curiosity shifted into glares, as if nothing had happened. Gertrude snapped, "Ew. Don't talk to us!"

Penelope added, "Yeah, you're soooo not my type." Both girls slammed their shoulders into Will as they walked past.

"What was that about?!" Will asked.

"It appeared to be a social interaction of the werewolf variety—" Linus started.

But Ivy quickly snapped, "*Utshay upway,*" in Pig Latin. Then she whispered, "Linus, I know this is new for you, but trust me—you do *not* want the whole school hearing you rave about monsters. Even if they're werewolves, they won't know it. Town curse, remember? Only Alphas and natural-born werewolves can see stuff. Look around."

Linus surveyed the hallway. One out of every ten students had a furry face, a tail, and black eyes, yet no one seemed to notice.

"Fascinating," Linus whispered. "Approximately ten percent of our peers have been turned."

"Yup, and also, yikes," Ivy said, a shiver running up her spine.

"It's not just the students either…" Will nodded toward some of the teachers, who were also newly changed. "The good news is there haven't been any deaths in the local news. So that means the werewolves are just biting people, turning them…"

"Swelling their ranks," Linus noted. "But to what end?"

"Maybe Ozzie is building an army," Ivy guessed.

The three friends gulped. "Oracle said werewolves are stronger and faster than people. If they had an army, they'd be unstoppable."

"Ozzie had Dr. Pamiver change all the animals in town into vampires," Will said. "Stands to reason Ozzie has someone else changing folks into wolves. But who?"

The math teacher walked down the hall. Gray fur poked

out of his sweater-vest and collared shirt and coated his neck, face, and arms. He held a handkerchief to his nose as he sneezed again and again. Will pointed. "Mr. Villalobos is a werewolf."

"Yeah, but I don't think Mr. Allergies is the Alpha type," Ivy snorted. "Whoever's in charge is going to be a total boss."

Linus huffed. "You don't think an intellectual could be in charge?"

"No way," Ivy said. "Haven't you ever watched a nature documentary? An Alpha has to be strong and tough. They have to be willing to do whatever it takes to stay in power. Smart folks aren't like that. They're too nice. And nice doesn't get first place."

"That's a naive perspective," Linus snapped. "Haven't you ever heard of 'mind above muscle'?"

"It's 'brain over brawn,' you dork," Ivy said. "And in a fight, muscle is going to win every time."

"Incorrect," Linus said. "A logical mind will win every time."

"You realize neither of you is making me feel better," Will said. "I'm not the smartest or the strongest. So no matter what, if I have to fight the Alpha at some point… I'm going to lose."

All through math class, Will stared at his teacher. The awkward Mr. Villalobos wore thick glasses over his gray-furred face. He kept sneezing and dropping the chalk. Will's gut told him Mr. Villalobos was innocent, but after Linus and Ivy's argument, he felt conflicted. After all, Dr. Pamiver was super nice and he turned out to be a vampire.

When the bell rang, all the students rushed out of the classroom. Except Will. He gathered his notebook slowly. Nerves dizzied Will's stomach and sweat wet his brow. When Mr. Villalobos turned his back to erase the chalkboard, Will leaped into the closet and closed the door only enough to leave a crack so he could spy through it.

Will watched the teacher erase the board, sneeze three times, then mutter to himself as he retrieved a tissue from his desk to blow his nose.

The teacher sniffed at the air. He made an appalled face. "Did someone bring an onion into my classroom?" He sniffed, his nose wiggling as he moved around the classroom toward the closet.

Will sniffed his hands. They still reeked of onions from when Ivy had tossed one at him earlier. Maybe this wasn't such a bright idea, Will thought. If his math teacher was the wolf Alpha, and Will got caught, he might be turned over to Ozzie.

The teacher kept sniffing, walking closer and closer to the closet until—his cell phone rang. He answered, "Hello, my love."

Mr. Villalobos turned his back to the closet. Will breathed a sigh of relief.

"Yes, dear. Yes, if you could buy more antihistamines, I'd truly appreciate it. My allergies have been just awful since someone started turning all these poor people into werewolves. Who would do such a thing? The wolf dander alone is unbearable. I much preferred when I was the only wolf in town, and a natural-born one at that—"

Will felt a wave of relief. Mr. Villalobos was innocent. With the teacher's back turned, Will stepped out of the closet slowly. He tiptoed to the door. He was almost there when the math teacher saw him. "Mr. Hunter?"

"Uh…" Will picked up a pencil on the floor. "Almost forgot this. I better get to my next class. Take care now!" Will ran out.

💀💀💀

Will was excited for his last class of the day: gym. Not because he enjoyed physical education, but because he shared the class with Linus and Ivy. Of the three of them, Ivy loved sports and physical activity. Will would have much preferred reading comics or playing video games, but he was fine with it. And Linus downright loathed exercise.

Wise Reader, consider that it is good to have an active mind as well as an active body. Many find it quite fun to throw rubber balls at other people in the game commonly referred to as dodgeball. I fully endorse this contest. What I do not endorse is throwing rocks at monsters. Many people have thrown rocks at me, and you know what? They hurt. A lot.

But as I was saying…

After he changed into his uniform, Will ran onto the court. He gave Ivy and Linus the good news about the innocent math teacher. "Guess we can cross him off our list of suspects. But what now?"

"We craft a new list of potential Alphas," Linus said.

"Right. We write down the name of every werewolf we see—starting with Coach Ewflower." Ivy nodded her head toward their gym teacher, who was sporting a light tan coat of fur on her face. "She wasn't like that last month. And she's as aggressive as they come."

"If only we knew what Ozzie's plan was…" Will whispered.

"Speak of the devil…" Ivy said, "or in this case, *witch*."

Standing in the gymnasium doors was Ozzie herself. She wore dark leather knee-high boots, a crimson corset, and long flowing velvet robes. Her purple hair was tied back in warrior braids and beads with Norse runes carved into them. On her shoulder sat the Franken-Hare, Faust.

The three friends froze, their veins flooding with fear. It was one thing to see—and battle—the ancient witch outside school, but to see her here? At school? It was too much. School was supposed to be a safe place. It appeared nowhere in East Emerson was safe.

Will's new wolfen sense made it so that he could smell her from across the room. She smelled of jasmine, pine, and smoke. There was also a sharper, more acrid scent… like magic.

As Ozzie strolled across the gym, she walked through a group of kids playing basketball. Too late, one of them passed the ball. It flew toward Ozzie's face. With catlike reflexes, she snapped her fingers, and the ball burst into flames. Other students opened their mouths in shock and gasped or cried out—before immediately forgetting, thanks to the town curse.

Faust leaped from her shoulder and flew above the students. No one noticed the winged hare or the witch—no one except Ivy, Linus, and Will, though they pretended not to. As far as Ozzie knew, she had erased their minds and they were as much under the town curse as the rest of the population.

The witch slowed her pace when her eyes locked on the trio.

Ivy quickly whispered, *"Illway, Inuslay, etendpray otnay otay eesay erhay. Actway ikelay I'mway ayingsay omethingsay unnyfay."* Then louder than usual, Ivy stammered, "—and then I said, 'Egypt City is definitely the capital of Egypt!' And the teacher said I was wrong! Can you believe it?!"

"Your teacher was correct," Linus said. "Cairo is the capital of Egypt."

Ivy elbowed her brother in the ribs, hissing in their secret language, *"Ayplay alongway, ummyday!"*

Linus caught on. They needed to ignore Ozzie. "Oh. OH! Yes, yes, that is an exceedingly humorous narrative," Linus said. "I have my own fantastic tale. The other day, Professor Jenkins incorrectly marked my exam. He'd given me credit for a question that I failed to answer correctly. When I pointed out his mistake, he said he just assumed

I'd gotten them all right. He wanted to give me the points anyway, but I insisted he take them off. Fair is fair after all."

"Wait, seriously?" Ivy asked her brother. "You told your teacher to take *off* points?"

"Honesty is a virtue," Linus replied.

"You know, for someone so smart, you can be really dumb," Ivy growled.

Ozzie's glance finally drifted away as she found Ewflower. Will watched out of the corner of his eye as the witch said to the coach, "We must speak."

"This is hardly the time or place," Ewflower snapped, agitated.

"If I say it is, *it is*," the witch commanded.

Ewflower glared at Ozzie. "Class. Start your warm-ups! I'll be right back."

"Dumb?" Linus continued. "My digitus minimus manus has vastly more intellect than every bone in your skeletal frame combined."

"Well, how smart are you going to be after I break your skull open with my fist?"

"Okay, Ozzie and Faust are gone," Will whispered. "Good cover, you two. You can stop pretending to argue."

Ivy and Linus scowled at Will at the same time, asking, "Who's pretending?"

"Ozzie is talking to Coach Ewflower," Will said. "We should follow them."

"True leaders require plans of action," Linus snapped. "The last time you two insisted on skipping a plan, Will ended up as a lycanthrope's chew toy."

"Plans are overrated," Ivy said. She got up and ran toward the hall, Will following just behind.

"Why does no one listen to me?" Linus groaned. He jogged to catch up.

Ivy put her finger up to her lips, signaling for quiet. The trio peeked around the corner. The corridor led to the locker rooms, the equipment closet, and the office for the gym teachers. The witch's boots *click-clack*ed against the floor as she followed Ewflower into her office.

"No way. Ewflower is involved with Ozzie? I never would have thought. She's so tough and no-nonsense. Did you know she's the first female coach to win state and national sporting trophies for East Emerson? Apparently, she was so focused on winning, her husband left her and took the kids."

"Sad," Linus whispered, "but why does that matter?"

Ivy shrugged. "I don't know. Just sharing."

A heated argument echoed out of the office, but the voices were too muffled to make out anything. Ivy made a closing-zipper motion across her lips to the other two. They nodded. Slowly, they stepped quietly toward the coach's office.

"—steal it yourself," Ewflower growled. "I'm not some errand wolf-girl, or a thief."

"You are what I say you are," Ozzie rasped. "Or have you forgotten your pledge to me and the Thirteen?"

"I haven't," Ewflower snapped. "But I made my vow when I thought we were going to be a powerful family, working together to attain absolute power. Instead, you keep all of us separate. I'm tired of working alone."

"You are hardly alone. You are the Alpha of a growing pack of wolves, one that will help me to accomplish our endgame."

"You mean *your* endgame," Ewflower sneered. "Simon is your heart's desire."

"And yours is a sense of belonging and victory," Ozzie sneered back.

"Well, we're hardly winning, are we? You lost Pamiver—"

"I didn't *lose* him. He betrayed us. He had to be punished."

"Betrayal is an indication of poor leadership. Every good coach knows that," Ewflower stated. "If he'd been happy, he wouldn't have strayed."

"Is that a threat? Did you forget who made you what you are now?" Ozzie hissed. "I made you, and I can unmake you. Or simply tear you asunder with my bare hands."

The coach laughed. "If you're so all-powerful, then why do you need the Thirteen at all? Why not do this all yourself?"

"*Just do as you're told!*" Ozzie shouted. Will noted the slightest edge of fear in the witch's voice. It was familiar, because that's how Will spoke lately too.

"I'm already building you an army. Isn't that enough?"

"*Just steal the book!*" Ozzie commanded.

"What book?" Linus whispered.

"*Shhh,*" Ivy hushed.

"*Meorw!*" the Franken-Hare mewed from the other side of the door.

"What is it, Faust?" Ozzie asked.

Will grabbed Ivy and Linus, yanking them backward into the equipment closet. He closed the door as quickly and quietly as he could, but it wouldn't shut. The tip of a jump rope stuck out by a single inch. They heard footsteps. There was nothing they could do now—except hide.

As he scanned the room, Will's sense of smell was overwhelmed. He wanted to puke. Instead, he realized there was only one solution: he and his friends dove into a large basket of dirty gym laundry, digging beneath the uniforms, underwear, socks, and wet towels. They'd barely covered themselves when the door swung open. The equipment closet was as quiet as a tomb except for the footsteps of the witch, Coach Ewflower, and the swish of Faust's wings until its paws found the ground. Then the footsteps hushed, and the only sound was the soft ticking coming from Faust's mechanical heart.

"*Rrrrwww!*" the Franken-Hare growled.

"Smells like onions in here," Ozzie hissed.

"Dirty gym clothes usually smell worse," the coach replied.

Will held his breath. He hoped the others did the same. If they were found out—game over. Ozzie had already warned them once.

The silence was deafening.

"It seems your beast was mistaken," Coach Ewflower snapped.

Ozzie slammed Ewflower into the wall, crushing the stone bricks behind her. "Who are you calling beast, *wolf*?"

A low, rumble rose in Ewflower's throat.

"Your orders are simple, Ewflower," Ozzie said. "Steal the book. Build the army. And have your wolves dig until Daednu can complete his crew for the excavation. I'll not hear another word from you—or you'll be replaced. Understood?"

Will, Ivy, and Linus didn't dare move while the adults were still nearby. They waited, listening to the *click-clack* of Ozzie's boots. Instead of walking toward the gym, her footsteps sounded in the other direction until there was a gnashing groan of metal grinding against stone. Whatever opened had closed again.

"Stupid witch," Ewflower muttered to herself. Then the coach stormed into her office and slammed the door.

Will, Ivy, and Linus all finally took a breath. Will thought he was going to retch from the stench filling his wolfen nostrils.

Ivy whispered, "Whoa, did you hear Ewflower stand up to Ozzie? I like her."

"Don't like her too much. She's one of the bad guys," Will whispered back as they crawled out of the laundry basket. "Ewflower is the Alpha. And now we know what she's doing."

"Building an army. Doing the digging. Stealing a book," Ivy whispered. "But an army for what? Digging where? And what book?"

Will covered his nose. "Can we go? I can barely breathe in here."

Linus sniffed. "All I smell is my onion."

"You kidding?" Ivy moaned. "We smell like jockstraps."

Will groaned. "You realize a wolf's sense of smell is a hundred times stronger than a human's? It stinks so bad, my eyes are watering."

"Perhaps we should pause the conversation until after we've made our escape?" Linus reminded the others in a hush.

The three kids crouched low, sneaking past Coach Ewflower's door. While Linus and Ivy made a beeline to return to class, Will hesitated. The hall led to a dead end. But he was certain that was the way Ozzie left. He could smell her, the smoke and magic, disappearing behind the wall. He tiptoed over to study the floor and the wall. He noticed three things.

One, several grooves were carved into the floor in an arc, as if the wall had opened up.

Two, he could feel an ice-cold and musty breeze coming in through the tiny cracks where the walls met... This was hiding some kind of door.

And, three, the bottom-right brick was marked with a familiar symbol:

VII

All over East Emerson, Will had discovered doors and wells marked with Roman numerals, which meant... "It's all connected—the wells and tunnels and doors—like some labyrinth or maze under the town," Will whispered to himself.

He pressed his hands and ear to the wall and heard the same drumming as last month: *buh-bum*, *buh-bum*, *buh-bum*. Like there was something alive, sleeping under East Emerson, something terrible, something so giant, so immense that its heartbeat could be heard for miles...

Chapter 4
the deadly librarian

✳

Will was walking Fitz. Each morning and evening he let the dog out in the backyard to do his business, but in the afternoons, he took Fitz for a long walk. It was part of their routine. Only today, the routine was going differently.

The Saint Bernard was walking and sniffing bushes. So was Will. Everything Fitz stopped to sniff, Will stopped to sniff as well. Then Fitz lifted his leg and peed on a bush. Then Will, not thinking the better of it, unzipped and, well…also *relieved* himself on the same spot.

Giggling Reader, you might think this comical. But for Will, it was awful. His body was changing in weird and mysterious ways, and those changes were making him act out in even weirder and more mysterious-er ways. Sometimes a person simply cannot help him- or her- or themself from acting on base instincts. Do not judge them too harshly. This happens to most people on a regular basis. (Especially teenagers.) Perhaps this has even happened to you. Why? Because ultimately, we're all animals.

Well, except for me. I'm a monster.

Will didn't even realize he was peeing in public until Ivy shouted, "Will!"

Will leaped behind the bush. "O-M-G, O-M-G, O-M-G. Please tell me I wasn't—"

"You were," Linus said. "It is…natural, I suppose. But perhaps…you know…do not make it a habit."

"I can't live like this," Will whispered. He rubbed his temples. "I thought Oracle's brew was supposed to help."

"Help you resist the call and commands of the Alpha. Not stop you from acting like a cute little canine," Ivy said. She patted his head.

"Are you petting me?" Will asked.

"Want me to scratch behind your ear? Who's a good boy?"

"Hilarious," Will groaned.

"Don't be *ruff*, neighbor. I'm sure what you're going through is *terrier*-fying." Ivy started laughing.

Linus shook his head at his sister. "Ivy, please. Will is becoming more of a *Canis lupus* with each passing moment. He does not need your insults on top of that."

"They're not insults, they're jokes," Ivy noted. "But you're right. Will could use a vacation. Perhaps we could go to *Howl*-lywood, California."

"You are not even funny," Linus said.

Ivy frowned. "But I spent all morning looking up dog jokes on the internet."

"Truly not helpful, sister." Linus patted Will's back. "We are going to fix this, Will. Grab your bike. Our little Supernatural Society is taking a field trip."

"Where are we going?" Ivy asked.

"To the one place with all the answers—" Linus stood up straight "—the local library."

💀💀💀

Like most towns, East Emerson had a small hotel, a post office, a café, and an antique store. Unlike other towns, East Emerson's small hotel was harassed by a seven-headed hydra. Its post office was a prison for pukwudgies and pegacorns (as in half pegasus, half unicorn). Its café catered coffee cake to centaurs. And its antique store was owned by three siren sisters who lured people in with their singing, then sweet-talked them into buying items they did not need—like possessed chandeliers, lamps that bit your fingers, and dolls with actual human baby teeth. (Nervous Reader, I too shivered at the thought of such horror.)

Yet unlike most places in East Emerson, the library was the most normal—

Pardon.

Dear Reader, might we pause for a moment to discuss—what exactly is *normal*? For me, normal is living out in the woods, battling banshees, and stopping the end of days on a daily basis. For you, normal is being smart and charming and reading scary books to brag to your friends that you read them. And for others, normal is…well, whatever they do day-to-day. The concept of *normal* is relative, meaning it completely depends on the person. But some use this word as a weapon, so much so that it is considered despicable to be *not normal*. Personally, I think being *not normal* is the best way to be.

So please, be careful when using the word *normal*. Don't use it to hurt another person's feelings. Or better yet, don't use it at all.

Now, back to the story…

Unlike most places in East Emerson, the library was ~~normal~~ like other libraries in other towns. The Emerson Library had books and computers and books and lamps and books and librarians and books and bookshelves and yes, more books. This library had books of every shape and size and age and was easily Linus's favorite place in the whole wide world. He came here so often that he knew each librarian by name, and they knew his as well.

Though there was one librarian whom he liked most of all—Ms. Dahlia Delphyne. To be honest, Linus had something of a crush on her. Though with that said, Linus had only ever seen Ms. Delphyne through the town curse—a woman in her early thirties with red hair who wore button-up sweaters and '70s-style glasses.

But today, as Linus walked through the front doors of his favorite place to see his favorite person, he was taken aback. With Oracle Jones's gift, Linus could see magical creatures as their true selves, which meant he was seeing Ms. Delphyne as her true self for the first time: She was still a woman in her early thirties with red hair who wore button-up sweaters and '70s-style glasses—but she was also a giant snake from the waist down. Oh, and she had terribly sharp fangs. (Though most lamias are known to devour children, the lamias of East Emerson aren't like that…anymore. These days, the only things they devour are books.)

Still, when Linus saw Ms. Delphyne, he screamed. Not like a little *"eek,"* but a whole guttural, primal *"ARGHHH-HHHHHH!!!"*

"Linus! Are you okay?!" Ms. Delphyne asked, slithering across the library.

Ivy punched her brother in the arm. *"Illchay, ittlelay otherbray. Eshay oesn'tday owknay ouyay ancay eesay erhay uetray ormfay."*

"Um. Oh. Uh…apologies, Dahlia… I mean Ms. Delphyne… I just, well, I stubbed my toe… Yes, that is what I did," Linus stuttered, trying not to look at her.

"It's okay. I did a little screaming myself this morning when I first came in," the lamia said, nodding around the library. "Look at this mess."

As Linus stepped past the lobby, he felt like screaming again. This time not out of terror, but devastation and upset. The library had been trashed. Tables and chairs were overturned, computers broken, and books scattered everywhere.

"What happened?" Will asked.

"Someone broke in last night," the librarian explained. "They ransacked the place. Worse, they had the gall to bring dogs with them. Muddy paw prints are everywhere."

Will sniffed the air. "You mean wolf prints."

"Did they take anything?" Linus asked.

"I don't know," Ms. Delphyne answered.

"There's nothing to steal from a library except—" Ivy started. Then she remembered. She shoved Linus and Will. "Ozzie told Coach: *Steal the book*. So Coach stole a book."

"But which book?" Will asked.

"What coach?" Ms. Delphyne asked.

The three friends looked to one another for a lie to save them. But none of them had one.

The librarian's stare turned into a glare. "I said, *what coach?* And what do you know about who broke in here?!" The librarian circled them, her long green serpent's tail enclosing them.

Linus didn't want to lie to her. He respected librarians too much. And as I mentioned earlier, he had a crush on this one. So, he said, "Ms. Delphyne, you might want to sit down—or um, how do serpents sit?"

"Excuse me?"

"Linus, don't—!" Ivy started, but too late.

"You may cease the performance, Ms. Delphyne. We can perceive your true physical form. We know you are a lamia."

The librarian roared, letting out a high-pitched shriek. "*You* did this to my library! You defiled my place of worship!"

"What? I would—" Before Linus could say *never*, the lamia's fury boiled over, and she whipped her tail, slapping Linus's legs out from under him. As Will and Ivy ran to defend him, her tail whipped again, throwing them across the library.

The lamia slithered behind the main desk and grabbed a sword and shield from below it. Then she wrapped around Linus like a boa does its victim. She roared, bearing her razor-sharp teeth, beating the sword against the shield. "Tell me what you've taken! Before I was a lover of books, I was a lover of war and death! And I can bring pain like no other!"

Green spittle splashed over Linus's face and glasses. She unhinged her jaw, as if about to swallow Linus whole.

"Get away from my brother, snake-lady!" Ivy pushed over a nearby bookshelf. It crashed down—right onto the tip of the librarian's tail.

"*Raaaawwwwwwwwwwwwwwwrrrrrrrrrrrrrrr!*" Ms. Delphyne cried.

The lamia dropped Linus and slid toward Ivy. She

wrapped around her. But as the librarian raised her sword, Will leaped onto the serpent's back. "Let Ivy go!"

Will held on tight as the half woman, half serpent bucked and bounced about like a rodeo bronco. Ms. Delphyne smacked Will with her shield. She then grabbed him with her tail and hoisted Will into the air, just above her mouth, her vicious fangs ready to tear him apart.

"Please, stop it, all of you!" Linus shouted. "Ms. Delphyne! Dahlia! We did *not* steal anything! Consider this logically. If we had successfully robbed the library last night, would we return this morning? And you know me. You know I would *never* commit such a crime. I've been coming here since I could first read. I love the library and would never disrespect or defile an honored monument of shared tomes. We came here seeking knowledge of our enemies, the same villains who we suspect wrecked the library, the same ones who changed my friend Will into a werewolf without his consent. Please, trust me. We are on the same side…"

Ms. Delphyne hesitated. "Then who did this to my library?"

"We suspect a teacher at our school, an Alpha of local lycanthropes, who is working for a witch named Ozzie, who—"

"Say no more. I know *Oestre*," Ms. Delphyne interrupted. "What do you know of her? Is she friend or foe to you?"

"Foe," Linus said. "She intends to do something terrible to our town—we don't know what exactly yet, but we are going to stop her."

After a long, tense moment, Ms. Delphyne released Will. She placed her sword and shield on a nearby table. "I apologize for attacking. It has been a long time since a natural human saw my true form and did not want to execute me. I…overreacted."

"Yeah, we noticed!" Ivy snapped. She yanked her brother aside. "Linus, you just outed us to a monster. She could tell every monster in town. That puts a huge target on our backs. And for all we know, *she* works for Ozzie. What were you thinking?"

"I was thinking logically, as logic dictates that if Ms. Delphyne worked for Ozzie, then Ozzie would have asked *her* for the book. Instead, the witch insisted Ewflower steal it—leading me to the rational conclusion that this lamia and its library are *not* aligned with the malevolent enchantress. And the enemy of our enemy is our ally."

"Well put, Linus Cross." Ms. Delphyne slithered across the floor, picking up fallen books as she did. "Oestre—Ozzie as some call her now—is no friend of mine. Or any of the lamia. We have suspected her ill intentions for East

Emerson since she first appeared. We even hired a witch to place magical wards on our library so that no other witch can enter. After all, this town is our refuge. We enjoy living here. We do not want to lose it."

"See," Linus said, poking his sister.

Ivy groaned. "Lucky guess."

"But how can you see me?" Ms. Delphyne asked, touching her tail. "And how are you mixed up against Ozzie? No, don't tell me. The less I know, the better."

"We need to know which book was stolen. Can you help us?" Linus asked.

"I can't. I'm sorry," the librarian said. "If Ozzie is involved in something, I need to stay as far away as possible. You should too. Linus, please, whatever you're mixed up in, forget about it. Avoid Ozzie. She's dangerous. Deadly."

"We're already aware," Ivy said.

Ms. Delphyne shook her head. "You three should go home. Let someone else handle this. Stay out of this, whatever this is."

"We wish we could," Will said. "But we can't. And you can't either now. If you can help us, you have to."

Ms. Delphyne shook her head. "Ozzie is too powerful, even for me and my sisters."

"Ms. Delphyne, please listen to me," Linus said. "If Oestre wins at whatever game she is playing, she may destroy East Emerson. That means our homes are not safe. Your home is not safe. If you can assist us, you must."

Ms. Delphyne hesitated.

"I know you care," Linus continued. "You have devoted yourself to this building of books, to safeguard their legacy, and to educate the next generation. If Ozzie succeeds, this library, this town, and all of its residents may be lost."

After a long minute, the librarian slithered to the front door, placed the CLOSED sign on the window, and locked the doors. "I can try. But tell no one. Ozzie is a juggernaut of dark magic and believes deeply in revenge for any who work against her. If she found out—"

Dread filled the lamia's eyes.

Linus took her hand gently. "Your secret is safe with us."

"As long as *our* secret is safe with you," Ivy added.

"Serpent's promise," Ms. Delphyne said. She extended her hand. Ivy shook it.

As they set about cleaning up the library, Linus asked, "How did you come to be here, in East Emerson?"

"My kind, the lamias, began as a ferocious race. Half serpent, half human, we were ostracized and feared. Eventually humans decided we were too monstrous to live, just because we enjoyed eating babies from time to time. They hunted us down, almost to the point of extinction. The last of us gathered under the ruins of Delphi and vowed to stop eating human children—"

"No more babies for brunch? Hard life," Ivy muttered.

"Make jest, but we were cursed by the gods. No other meat or fruit would satisfy us but the flesh of children. After centuries of succumbing to baser instincts, we decided starving was a better alternative. We lived in caves, hoping to die. Instead, we ended up conquering our appetites. Eventually, we learned of East Emerson—a town cursed to *not* see the supernatural. On this island, no one can see what we really are. Here, we have a fresh start, a chance to redeem ourselves. Here, my sisters and I pride ourselves on being architects of learning and the protectors of knowledge. We want to be better. Not every monster wants to *be* a monster."

"I understand that," Will said, looking at his own fur-covered hand.

Despite the tail and the fangs, Ms. Delphyne was still the same intelligent, compassionate librarian Linus had always had a crush on. And so the crush remained.

"Is that graffiti?!" Linus asked, appalled, pointing to a carving in the stone over the front doorway.

Nemo pythonissam et incantamentum
intrare potest hic,
uel patitur ignem aeternum.

"No," Ms. Delphyne said. "It's the protection spell I spoke of, to keep witches out. Placed there by a woman named Oracle Jones."

"You know Oracle?" Ivy asked.

"How did I never see that?" Linus asked before remembering that he'd only just received his supernatural sight. He began to wonder what else he had missed seeing before.

Realizing what the spell meant, Will said, "Witches *can't* come in here—which is why Ozzie sent Ewflower to steal the book."

"If only my books were in order, I could tell you what was missing," the lamia librarian noted. "I have a photographic memory."

Linus considered. "How good is it? If we lined up all the books, even out of order, could you figure out what was missing?"

"Of course! But we would need to get every book off the floor and onto a shelf, so I can see all the titles on the spines."

"That'll take hours," Ivy said.

Will thought about it. "Hold on. I don't think Ozzie's going to want a copy of a book she could buy online or at a store. She probably needs a special book. What about the ones you keep locked upstairs?"

"The old and rare editions in the attic. Of course." Ms. Delphyne led the others to the back door, which had been ripped off its hinges. The old, musty room's shelves lay sideways on top of one another, like knocked-over dominoes.

As the librarian looked around, something in Will's gut led him to the back, to the keyhole-shaped door, where a single book was housed, the one Ivy and Linus had shown him last month. That door too had been kicked open. Inside, the table was bare.

Linus looked over his shoulder. "No. The *PERDITIT HISTORIA RERUM*—*The History of Lost Things*—that's the book they stole."

"I don't understand," Ms. Delphyne said. "A library is for borrowing books. They didn't have to steal it. They could have just come in here and read it."

"Unless they didn't want anyone else reading it," Will said.

"I love that book," Linus admitted. "There's something about it, with its ancient languages and stories and the maps and the drawings. I even loved the smell of the crisp pages and the leather binding—"

"Oh, it's not leather," Ms. Delphyne said. "It's human skin."

Linus gulped. *Skin?*

"If Ozzie wants that book, we need to get it back," Will said. "Maybe Coach Ewflower hasn't given it to her yet. Maybe we can get it first."

"Then we better go," Ivy said.

The lamia took a deep breath. "I can't fight Ozzie overtly, but perhaps I can help in some other way?"

Linus smiled. "Could you research lycanthropy and search for anything about cures, treatments, or antidotes?"

"That, I can do," the lamia said.

"Then it's up to us to get that book back," Linus said.

Will, Ivy, and Linus returned outside to their bikes. "Are we really going to take on the Alpha wolf by ourselves?"

Ivy smiled and cracked her knuckles. "As long as we don't get caught, we'll be fine. Just follow my lead."

"You get caught all the time," Linus noted.

Ivy swallowed. "Right. Well, let's hope all that practice pays off now. Otherwise, we're werepuppy chow."

Chapter 5
The bungled burglary

✳

Dear Reader, you might be asking yourself, "Why on earth are Will, Ivy, and Linus hiding behind those shrubs?" Well, Clever Reader, when spying upon an adult werewolf mixed up in the dealings of an ancient and powerful and wicked witch, it is best to use extreme caution. This equates with staying out of sight, lurking in shadows, and not getting caught. So, when our three heroes decided to spy on Coach Ewflower to find the stolen book, all three agreed to not be spotted. And *that* is why our three heroes were hiding behind shrubs located at the back of the school's faculty parking lot.

"There she is," Will whispered. He pointed to a large muddy 4x4 Jeep. The friends waited while Coach Ewflower parked, grabbed her duffel bag, and disappeared inside the school. "Okay, now's our chance. Let's hurry."

Will, Ivy, and Linus raced across the parking lot. They were hunched over, and their heads were down—though Linus's backpack was so big, it would have been easily spotted if anyone knew to be watching. As soon as they got to the Jeep, Ivy tried one of the doors, and it popped right open.

"Good thing she doesn't believe in locking her car," Will noted as he climbed into the back seat, while Ivy and Linus took the driver's and passenger seats.

Ivy set her hands on the wheel. "I want a Jeep when I learn to drive."

"Focus," Linus snapped. "Ivy, search under the seats and in the side pockets. I'll investigate the glove compartment and this side. Will, check the back and the trunk. Be diligent in your exploration."

"You're not the boss of me," Ivy said.

"No, but I am the smartest person here. Now quiet your mouth hole and search before we get caught," Linus growled.

Ivy found herself impressed by her brother's commanding nature.

Will said, "Nothing back here except sports equipment."

"Nothing up here either," Ivy said.

"Same," Linus said.

"So, what now?"

"Maybe it was in the duffel bag she took with her," Will guessed. "Would it be smart to check her office?"

"Smart, no. Logical, yes," Linus stated. "When?"

"Lunchtime," Ivy said. "Coach Ewflower has to monitor the cafeteria on Tuesdays. She'll be away from her office for at least twenty minutes."

"Okay, then let's meet outside the gym after the lunch bell rings."

"Then when will we consume our midday sustenance?" Linus asked. "Eating a balanced diet at lunch is vital to productivity."

"Guess you'll just have to be stupid this afternoon," Ivy said.

Linus sighed. "The things I do to keep this town safe."

💀💀💀

When the lunch bell rang, the students of East Emerson Middle School raced to the cafeteria. Hungry Reader, as you probably know, lunchtime at school can be very stressful. First you must find something to eat. Then you must find a place to sit while you eat. It's not so much the eating that is hard as it is the sitting with a person or persons with whom you can have pleasant conversation. This is often difficult because children can be cruel, mean, and…well…monstrous.

I should know. In my youth, I briefly attended a secret school for monsters located deep under the canals of Venice, and the worst part? It was not the long hours of boring lectures or going to a bathroom with no stalls for privacy, no—it was the lunch itself. No one wanted to sit with me, and no one wanted me to sit with them. They called me names, made jokes at my expense, and threw potatoes at my oversize head. Some bit me, others fought me, a few even tortured me. Yet that physical agony was nothing compared to the hurt my heart endured at the verbal taunts of my peers. I've heard children do this every single day in regular human schools as well. So, Sweet Reader, my heart goes out to you if you've experienced this for yourself.

But worry not. Will and Ivy and Linus didn't have to deal with such nonsense today. Instead, they skipped lunch and met outside the gymnasium as planned to break into their teacher's office and retrieve a stolen book.

"I passed Ewflower in the hallway," Will noted. "She was on her way to the cafeteria."

"Rad. The clock is ticking," Ivy said, rubbing her hands together. "Let's do this."

"Sister, must you enjoy doing bad things so much?" Linus asked.

"Of course," Ivy said. As soon as they arrived at Coach Ewflower's office, they found a locked door. But Ivy used her set of metal tools to take care of it. "Ta-da! Ten points to me, the coolest girl in school."

"Gloat later. We must hurry," Linus said, brushing past. Once the three were inside the office, they locked the door and began searching through the cabinets and shelves, looking for the stolen library book.

"I don't see it," Ivy said, shutting the last of the cabinets.

"Me either," Linus noted, going through the last of the boxes next to the shelf.

"And it's not in her desk," Will said. "I even found the duffel she brought in. It's not in there either. It's just a bunch of junk mail and some overdue bills." Will's pointed ears perked up an inch. He whispered, "Footsteps."

"I don't hear anything," Ivy said.

Will's wolf nose started twitching. "I smell someone coming—they ate the meat loaf special for lunch."

Ivy examined her friend. "You look more doggish. Didn't you drink your antiwolf brew this morning?"

"Of course I did," Will hushed. "But who cares, we have to hide—NOW!"

The brother and sister crowded under the coach's large metal desk. Will hid behind the door as someone put a key into the lock. The door opened. All three friends held their breaths.

A man walked in, a jack-o'-lantern resting on his shoulders instead of a head. He mumbled angrily under his breath as he pushed a mop around on the floor. "...rather be back in the demon well. It's a lot better than cleaning up after these punks. But noooo... I had to set out on my own, thinking I'd become an actor. Why didn't I go to Hollywood?"

After a quick, sloppy mop, the school janitor left.

"Whew!" Ivy whispered. "Let's get out of here before Ewflower gets back."

"But the book—" Linus started.

"—isn't here," Ivy finished.

"Wait," Will said, grabbing the electric bill from the duffel bag. "Now we have Ewflower's home address."

"Are you suggesting we burgle her home?!" Linus looked like he might pass out. "Breaking and entering is a *felony*. I cannot have illegal activity on my public record if I want to be accepted into an Ivy League university."

"College?" Wrapping her arm around Linus's neck, Ivy kissed her brother's forehead. "Oh, sweet brother of mine. At the rate we're going, we probably won't even survive middle school."

💀💀💀

As soon as the final school bell rang, they'd raced over on their bikes. "This is it," Will said, matching the address to the letter he held in his hand.

"And look! It's the same pink house from the last full moon," Ivy said, "where those Neighborhood Watch creeps turned into wolves. Wait, do you think—I bet Ewflower called them over, then bit them in her backyard."

"All the more reason *not* to do this," Linus stated. "It is dangerous—and morally wrong."

"We're stealing a book that she stole first. You can't steal stolen goods from a thief," Ivy stated. Then she scratched her head. "Can you?"

"I suppose there are philosophical merits to both sides of the argument—" Linus started, but Ivy quickly placed her hand over his mouth.

"Stop talking. You hang outside and keep watch. If anyone comes, give us a signal."

"You want me to stay outside *alone*?" Linus asked. "Absolutely not."

"Fine. Then come with," Ivy said, "but leave your backpack with the bikes. It's only going to get in the way."

"My go bag comes with me," Linus said. "What if there's an emergency?"

"Like taping your mouth shut?" Ivy mocked.

"I do have three different kinds of tape," Linus answered, "all chosen specifically because they are strong enough to keep even you from yapping."

"Are we doing this or not?" Will asked. "Ewflower could come home any minute. It's now or never. Ivy, can you do your lock-trick thing on her door?"

"Only if necessary," Ivy said. She snuck up to the front door, lifted up the doormat, and revealed a key. "Yeesh. People always think this is such a good place to hide the spare key. Bunch of dummies."

Ivy unlocked the door and the three entered the dark

front room. "The house isn't too big, but we should split up. Will, take the kitchen and living room. Linus, check out the office, the bathroom, and the hall closet. I'll check the bedrooms. Remember, don't turn on the lights. Use the flashlights Linus brought."

The three friends went their separate ways. Sneaky Reader, when investigating a villain's home, it is never a good idea to split up. Though it is a good idea to hurry, which sometimes necessitates splitting up. My advice? Do your best to not be in a position where you have to investigate a villain's home in order to save the town. It will make your heart race, your palms sweat, and give your writer (and your readers) a very nervous feeling.

Also, do us both a favor, and do *not* break into your teacher's home. This will get you into trouble, and me as well. You might go to prison, which—if my time in a Russian gulag is any indication—is not a pleasant experience. Plus, have you ever been hounded by the legal system? That's even worse than being burned at the stake, then drowned because you didn't die. I've done that too, and it's not nearly as miserable as the paperwork and debt created by lawyers.

Where was I? Oh, yes.

As Will turned the first corner, a massive eagle appeared, claws extended. He barely grabbed his mouth in time to stifle a scream. The bird didn't move. Like the rest of the animal heads on the wall, the eagle was taxidermic. Everywhere Will's light flashed, there were more teeth, more claws, and more reflective marble eyes watching him. The quicker they got out of here, the better.

Will went through the kitchen cabinets, pantry, and looked in the fridge. He even found himself sniffing, just like a dog. No sign—or smell—of the book. In the living room, he checked behind the couch, under the cushions, and all of the bookshelves. He found nothing. As he turned to leave, he noticed a large framed photo on the wall. It was Coach Ewflower as he'd never seen her—smiling. She sat in the middle of a family portrait, her husband standing behind her, and her two children beside her.

A deep well in Will's stomach ached as he considered his dad.

He thought of what Ivy told him about Ewflower: she'd been so focused on work and winning that her husband left and took their kids. As Will stared at the photo, he wondered why his dad hadn't taken him. It wasn't that he didn't want to be with his mom, but his dad hadn't even tried or argued about it. Will remembered the night he'd heard that moment from his bedroom in Brooklyn, Dad saying to Mom in the kitchen: "You take Will. I can't."

Why couldn't he? Will wondered. The ache in his stomach spread, making his whole body hurt.

"Find anything?"

Will almost screamed again, but Ivy threw her hand over his mouth in time. She whispered, "It's only me, dogbreath."

"I didn't find anything," Will said.

"Me either," Linus said, joining the others.

"Where could the book be then?" Ivy groaned. "It's not in her Jeep, not in her office, not in her home… It has to be here somewhere."

Will sniffed the air. "Do you smell that?"

"It's just me and Linus's onion fragrance," Ivy said.

"No, not that," Will answered. "The gross musty smell, like an old basement full of…*sniff*…of dirt and…*sniff*…mold."

Ivy and Linus sniffed and sniffed. "I smell nothing of the sort," Linus said. "But a human's nose has less olfactory receptors than a dog. Not to mention the portion of their brain designated for analyzing such smells—"

Ivy interrupted, "Linus, focus! Will, keep sniffing. Is there a hidden basement?"

Will's wolfen nose was twitching every which way. "Yes. I smell Coach Ewflower, I smell remnants of the school gymnasium, I smell leftover takeout for one…but also… the public library?"

"As in the library book we're looking for!" Ivy patted Will's head. "Good boy! Follow that scent."

Will growled. He got on all fours and sniffed, his nose wiggling and wrinkling. He followed right, then left, then right again, then over a large rug in the hallway. He nudged it aside, pushing the carpet back to reveal a trapdoor.

"I think Will's new wolf powers are starting to work in our favor," Ivy said. She opened the door and crawled down the ladder into the dank basement. "Come on."

Their flashlights lit along the walls. One side of the room was dedicated to shelves and stacks of boxes marked HOLIDAY DECORATIONS or FAMILY PHOTO ALBUMS. The other side was decorated with placards and cases of sports trophies. There were dozens of athlete medals, including an Olympics bronze medal hanging from a photo of Coach Ewflower on a stage accepting the award.

Ivy was impressed. "Wow. She must have been something special in her day."

Linus shrugged. "Personally, I do not see the appeal in sports."

"The Olympics isn't just sports, dude. It's the best of the best in the world. Those people devote their entire lives to a single feat. It's amazing."

Will whispered, "Yeah, but no matter how much you love something, you shouldn't give up your family for it."

"What's that?" Ivy asked. On the back wall, a dark cloak hung on a black hook.

Will sniffed. "It reeks of bonfire smoke." A memory came rushing back. "The first night I was in Emerson, the silver fox lured me to the cemetery to watch Ozzie try to conjure up and speak to Simon. The Thirteen were there, wearing these robes. Guess Coach Ewflower is one of them."

"Does it really surprise you that a teacher is evil?" Ivy asked.

"Just because one teacher is evil does not mean all teachers are evil," Linus replied. "I happen to regard my educators with the highest praise and respect. I suspect you do not because you earn bad grades."

"Or maybe teachers just don't like me," Ivy said.

"Perhaps they do not respect you because you do not do your homework," Linus replied.

"That's…fair," Ivy noted.

"Look at this," Will said. There was a marble trunk below the robe. Will sniffed around it. "The library book is in there. I can smell it."

Ivy tried to open it, but it wouldn't budge. She grabbed a crowbar from a nearby toolbox and tried to wedge it open. She tried with all her might, but the trunk was locked. Linus flashed his light over the box's peculiar engravings:

15-14-12-25 19-08-5 15-18 08-05
23-09-20-08 23-15-12-06'19 02-12-15-15-04
18-21-14-14-09-14-07 09-14 20-08-05-09-18
22-05-09-14-19
13-01-25 15-16-05-14 20-08-09-19 03-08-05-19-20.

"It's another code," Will noted. He pulled the golden pyramid from his pocket. "But this one is all numbers—it doesn't match Pamiver's key stone either."

"Who cares," Ivy said. "Help me try to open this."

Linus and Ivy both used all of their combined strength. Even with the use of the crowbar, the lid wouldn't budge. Ivy started to hit the trunk with the crowbar. "Open, dang you!"

"Stop!" Will hushed. "You're being loud. Let me try." He stared at the numbers… "Look, none of the numbers go over 25. There's only 26 letters in the alphabet. What if this is a new cipher, where A=1 and Z=26?"

"Got pen and paper?" Ivy asked her brother.

"Of course," he said, pointing to his backpack. "Third pocket on the left."

Quickly, Linus wrote out the code and Ivy decoded. But before they could finish, Will reached over. His finger barely grazed the lid, and it slid open.

"How the heck—?!" Ivy started.

Inside the trunk was the library book *The History of Lost Things*. "I look forward to returning you to your rightful home with Ms. Delphyne." Linus picked up the book and kissed it.

Ivy smirked. "Didn't she say that cover was made of human skin?"

Linus gagged, then wiped his lips.

Will was about to shut the chest when a gold glint caught his eye.

Under two stacks of cash, a passport, and an old pistol was a familiar shape—a small golden pyramid. It was the same shape and size as Pamiver's but was covered in different symbols. The bottom had a wheel too, except instead of two alphabets, it had an alphabet that aligned with the numbers one through twenty-six. Will was right about the cipher.

"Another key stone," Will whispered to his friends.

"Pocket it," Ivy said, "we need to jet." She pushed the others up the ladder and into the living room. She closed the trapdoor, replaced the rug, and rushed toward the front door. As they were about to leave, Coach Ewflower's Jeep pulled into the driveway out front. "Back door! Go go go!"

"There *is* no back door," Will said.

"Back bedroom then, and out the window!"

The three ran into the farthest bedroom and quickly, quietly, closed the door. Will flipped the lock, just to be sure—and just in time. They heard the front door open and shut. Will tiptoed to the window. It refused to open. He examined it. It was nailed shut. He waved his arms frantically, mouthing the words, *What do we do now?!*

Ivy and Linus studied the room, as if some new exit might appear. Will's eyes went wide. He whispered, "I can smell the coach."

Ivy shrugged. "So?"

"If I can smell her, then she can smell *us*."

Moving faster than thought, Ivy grabbed a perfume bottle on the nearest cabinet and started spritzing herself, Linus, and Will.

"What are you doing?!" Will hissed.

"Making sure she can't sniff us out, now or later," Ivy whispered. "All she'll smell is her own perfume."

"I smell like my mom," Will groaned.

"Better than smelling *dead*," Ivy retorted, "which we'll all be if we're found here."

"You know, I may not be able to smell you, but I can

certainly *hear* you," Coach Ewflower announced from the other side of the door. The doorknob wiggled. "You have ten seconds to explain who you are and what you're doing in my house before I kick down this door. One…two…"

Will, Ivy, and Linus stared at each other with wide eyes. What were they going to do?

Dear Reader, if you ever find yourself trapped in the house of a lycanthropic villain and have only ten seconds to consider a way to escape a room, I suggest you take a deep breath and try not to panic. Of course, it's only a suggestion and rarely works in real life. Panicking is a natural response to such a situation. Luckily for our heroes, Will felt anxious all the time since his parents' divorce. So rather than panic, he considered his options.

"…three…four…"

Quickly, Will opened Linus's backpack and found what he needed. He pulled out the Mace spray and the pantyhose.

"…five…six…"

Will pulled the nylon tights over his face, stepped next to the door, and aimed the sprayer.

"…seven…eight…nine…" Coach Ewflower kicked open the door early. She wasn't sure what she expected to see, but it certainly was not a wolf-boy holding a can of Mace and whose face was squished into weird brown shapes by pantyhose.

"You forgot to say *ten*." Will squeezed the trigger and Mace shot out into the coach's eyes.

She screamed, clutching her own furry face, burning foam dripping from her black eyes. Her whole body began to shake and twist and change. Her tan fur grew longer, thicker. Then her knees snapped backward, and new joints appeared. Her muscles swelled, bones broke and reshaped, her whole body doubling in size. She collapsed onto the ground, then stood again—this time as a fully turned werewolf.

She howled and sniffed at the room, her eyes still blinded by the Mace. She launched herself at Will. Ivy tackled him, knocking him out of the way just in time as the wolf crashed into a mirror.

Ivy wanted to make a crack about seven years of bad luck. But now wasn't the time. Instead, she shoved Linus and Will out of the bedroom, down the hall, and outside the front door. They hopped on their bikes, and pedaled as fast as they could go. As they turned the corner at the end of the street, they looked back and saw a wolfen Coach

Ewflower run out of her house. Still, holding her eyes, she sniffed the air and started running toward them.

"She can smell us!" Ivy cried.

"This way," Will shouted. He yanked the pantyhose from his face. He turned one corner, and then the next, his friends following close. He guided his bike over a low bridge, then at the last second, turned to the right. He and his bike flew down the shallow ravine and into the chilly saltwater stream. Ivy and Linus followed. They didn't whisper, they didn't make a peep. They heard growls and snarls as Ewflower approached, then the sound of a heavy beast on the wooden bridge overhead. The werewolf sniffed. Sniffed again.

As if the weather knew, a huge gust of wind came along, blowing from the other direction. Alpha wolf Coach Ewflower howled, "I'll find you, brats. And I'll make you pay!" Then she took off running in the other direction. Just to be on the safe side, the three friends waited in the cold water for the next twenty minutes before moving an inch.

💀💀💀

"Stop! No more!" Linus screamed. "This is torture!"

"What he said!" Will screamed. "No more! It's freezing! Is this what ice cream feels like all the time?!"

Ivy laughed. She was enjoying herself far too much. Both boys stood in their underwear as Ivy sprayed them down in Will's backyard with a water hose. It was November, and the northeastern fall weather wasn't designed for outdoor soakings.

"Sorry, boys—" Ivy smirked "—you don't want to go inside smelling like middle-aged women, do you? I can, but our parents will have way too many questions if you do."

"At this point, I'm willing to risk it," Will pleaded, his teeth and fangs chattering so hard he thought they might break. "I want soap and shampoo and *hot* water…"

"Where's the fun in that?" Ivy asked. She squeezed the trigger harder, spraying them with more frigid water.

Will jumped away and then shook his whole body, just like Fitz would. The cold water splashed Ivy and she screamed. Linus pointed and laughed. "Hah!"

"So, little brother," Ivy asked, turning the hose on him again, "are we going to talk about the pantyhose?"

Linus's lips quivered as he tried to answer. "Pantyhose have a vast amount of uses—as ties, nets, patches, containers, even to find lost objects by putting the pantyhose over the end of a vacuum cleaner, or use as a sieve. As such, I included a pair in my go-bag for odds and ends uses. And good thing I did. With one over his face today, Will was unrecognizable."

"So, you think we got away with it? Coach didn't see our faces?" Ivy asked.

"No way," Will said. "She couldn't have. I maced her as soon as the door opened."

Will sniffed himself. Then he sniffed Linus and Ivy. His smile fell. "She won't need to see us to recognize us."

"But how?" Ivy asked. "I doused us in *her* perfume. At her house, she would have only smelled herself."

"Exactly," Will said. "Like Linus said earlier, a dog's sense of smell is extraordinary—which I'm learning firsthand. You and Linus may not be able to smell the perfume, but I still can. And so will Coach Ewflower. Tomorrow, when we go to school, she'll sniff us out by the scent of her own fragrance, and then—"

Will dragged his finger across his throat. "—the end."

Chapter 6
the lost things in the lost book

✳

"Guillermo, it's time to get up," said Ms. Vásquez, knocking on the bedroom door as she opened it. "You slept through your alarm. Twice. Come on, you don't want to be late for school."

Will didn't get out of bed. He coughed. "I'm trying but I… I just feel so weak." He sat up slowly and coughed again. "Is it hot in here?"

Mom placed the back of her hand on her son's forehead. "Uh-oh. You're burning up. And you're all sweaty. Stay in bed. I'm afraid no school for you today."

"But I have a vocabulary quiz—I need to go."

Will's mom looked surprised. "You *want* to go to school? That's a first."

"School's not so bad. *Cough*. Plus, we're watching this film series in science *cough* about animals all around the world. *Cough*. It's pretty neat."

"I'm glad you want to learn, but you're feverish. I'll call the school and let them know you aren't coming. Try to go back to sleep."

"But, Mom—"

"No arguments," she said. "I have to go to work, but I'll call and check on you, okay? Just rest. And drink plenty of fluids."

"Okay," Will said.

As soon as his mom closed the door, Will winked at Fitz. His dog crawled under the blankets and pulled out a washcloth soaked with hot water. Using their walkie-talkies, Will called his friends. "Ivy, your plan worked like a charm."

"Duh, I know," she said through the receiver. "I'm a professional when it comes to getting out of school."

Linus's voice broke in. "Behold, ladies and gentlemen: my sister, an exemplary example of the model student."

"Whatever. Skipping school to save the whole town is a good reason," Ivy said, "not to mention if Ewflower smells us and realizes we broke into her house, she's going to murder us. So yeah. Now, everyone pretend to rest until all of our parents go to work. Then, Will, head over here."

Innocent Reader, please know that I do not suggest skipping school. Education is important. I should know—I never had one, and now I'm a monster. Do you want to be a monster? I did not think so. Go to school.

Will waited until his mom's car pulled out of the driveway. Then he raced from his window to the shower—scrubbing himself three times over until the smell of perfume was gone—brushed his teeth, and put on clean clothes. He ran downstairs, poured Fitz a bowl full of kibble, and noticed Mom had left a note: **Feel better. Call me at work if you need anything. Te amo por siempre.**

Guilt boiled up in Will's stomach. He pushed it down. He hated lying to Mom, but she would never understand if she knew the truth.

Next to the note was Mom's phone. As soon as he picked it up, he considered calling his dad. He stared at the screen. Scrolling through the recent call history, he saw dozens of outgoing calls…all to his father. But no return calls. No missed calls. No voice mails.

Will took a deep breath and whispered to himself, "If he wants to call, he'll call."

A wave of anxiety hit him at the thought that his father might never call. But Will pushed that down too. Right now, he had other things to worry about—like the fate of East Emerson.

💀💀💀

Linus looked out the living room window for the third time.

"Cut it out," Ivy said. "If Ewflower was onto us, we'd be wolf toast by now."

"Wolf toast?" Will asked.

"You know, like avocado toast."

"That makes little to no sense," Linus stated. "By your comparison, that would mean mashed-up wolf on toast. How would we be that?"

"Oh. I meant wolves would eat us. I guess we'd be people-toast, or maybe regular toast. I don't know. What do wolves eat? Dog food? Will?"

"I do not eat dog food," he said. "Yet."

"Look, we've all showered, like, a dozen times, and Will says he can't smell the perfume on us anymore. We're good," Ivy said. "Let's stop worrying about Coach Wolf-Lady and start figuring out why she and Ozzie want this book so bad."

The trio gathered around the large tome titled *The History of Lost Things*. Linus turned page after ancient page with gentle care, examining dozens of handwritten entries, bizarre sketches and illustrations, and maps.

"So what is this book anyways?" Will asked, looking over his friend's shoulder. "When you first showed it to me, I thought it was just, like, some old history book."

"It is and it isn't, and it is so much more," Linus noted. "The part I showed you is toward the end—journal entries written by a Viking named Emer the Red. I suspect someone gave him the book, because if you go back before his handwriting starts, there's different entries in different languages. Going backward, we have Latin, Arabic, Mayan, Sanskrit, Tamil, Aramaic, Old Chinese, Mycenaean Greek, Egyptian, and Sumerian."

"Whoa. Sumerian is the oldest known written language, dating back to 3100 BC," Ivy said, tracing her finger over a page. "The earliest evidence of the language was found in the Kish Tablet, a limestone found in Iraq. The writing was pictographic—you know, speaking through pictures. Basically, the earliest form of emojis."

Linus and Will stared at Ivy in disbelief.

"What? I told you I'm good with languages."

Linus smiled. "And here you thought you were just the brawn of the group. You are far smarter than you give yourself credit for. If you just applied yourself at school—"

Ivy put her hand over her brother's mouth. "Shhh. Don't ruin the fun for me."

"So if this book is so old, shouldn't it be in the Smithsonian or the American Museum of Natural History? What's it doing here in East Emerson?"

"An excellent question," Linus said. "I hypothesize the book is tied to this town somehow and, perhaps, also linked to the supernatural." Linus traced his finger down the side of the book, asking, "But why would Ozzie demand Ewflower steal it?"

As if a wind filled the room, the pages began to turn on their own. Only there was no wind. Hundreds of pages flipped from left to right...

"How—? Did you—?" Linus stuttered.

"What'd you do, Linus?" Ivy snapped.

"Nothing! I don't know! The book is moving on its own, which is obviously *impossible*."

"Nothing is impossible," Will said, "not in this town."

The pages slowed and then stopped, landing on a large

diagram. It was a circle inside a triangle inside a circle inside a triangle inside a circle inside a triangle.

"I know that symbol," Will whispered. He fumbled to pull the golden pyramid out of his pocket. "Look. It's on here. But what is it?"

Ivy shrugged. "I'm good at languages, not geometry."

"It is not math," Linus stated, taking a closer look at the book. "The handwriting is by the narrator, known as Artemis. I've translated some of her journal entries. She claimed to be a witch and went on to marry Emer. The designs are some kind of formula or equation, maybe a spell of some kind?"

"'Quam ad captionem et carcerem serpens Deus sub in fine mundi,'" Ivy read. "Something about…jailing a serpent…a god…under…the end of the world?"

A shiver rushed up Ivy's spine. Linus's scalp tightened. And Will felt as though he'd been dropped into a pool of ice water.

Will noticed the next page was thicker than the other pages. Carefully, he pulled on it. The page folded out, once, twice, again and again, until the paper revealed it was twelve times as long as the book. It was an etched drawing of a massive serpent, the size of a dinosaur. And under it was written the word that Will had seen again and again since moving to this town: JÖRMUNGANDR.

"Remember when Ozzie was going to kill us," Will whispered. "She said we belong to East Emerson, and East Emerson belongs to *Simon and his serpent*."

"What does that mean?" Linus asked. The three friends exchanged clueless looks.

The front door's knob jiggled. Will and Ivy froze in panic, while Linus dove behind the couch. "Coach Ewflower found us!"

The door opened. Mr. Cross stood there, raising an eyebrow. "Well, it looks like my kids are feeling well enough to have a guest over on their sick day."

Ivy stammered to explain, "Oh, well, see, um—"

Linus's face flushed bright red. "Please do not ground me, Dad! I wanted to go! You know I love education! It was Ivy's idea to skip school. Not mine!"

"Way to throw me under the bus," Ivy snorted.

"Son, take a deep breath," Mr. Cross chuckled. "You're playing hooky today, huh? Why didn't you just say so?"

"Huh?" Ivy asked.

"Huh?" Linus repeated.

"Look, I get it. Everyone needs a break from time to

time." Mr. Cross closed the door and took off his shoes. "But I don't like lying. Next time, just tell me you need a day off."

"Whoa. Coolest dad ever," Will whispered to his friends.

"I mean, yeah, I guess he's alright," Ivy said, even as she smiled.

Will wondered how his dad would handle the situation. Mr. Hunter had always been so cool in the past, so he'd probably say something similar. But if Dad was so laid-back, why hadn't he called? Was he hurt? Had something bad happened to him? Or had he just stopped caring? The familiar pit opened up in Will's stomach, and he felt his worry crawling over him like spiders.

Mr. Cross held up a large brown paper bag. "I left work early to bring home some chicken noodle soup, but I'm guessing you'd rather have pizza. How about I make lunch and we have a movie-on-the-couch afternoon?"

"*Daaaaaaad*," Ivy whined, "we're not five anymore."

"Actually, I think that sounds nice," Will said. He felt his anxiety retreating at the very thought of a normal afternoon.

"What about our...you know...*homework*," Linus whispered, secretly meaning the mystery at hand.

"It can wait," Will said. "I mean, we have to eat, right? Here, Mr. Cross. I'll help you."

Ivy and Linus glanced at one another, confused and annoyed. But Will didn't care. His friends may not appreciate their father, but he certainly did.

💀 💀 💀

As they ate, Ivy and Linus sat on one couch while Mr. Cross and Will sat on the second. Will and his friends' father were watching a comedy movie, both laughing at all the same corny jokes. Ignoring the TV, Linus examined the old book, taking notes on a yellow pad while also researching on his laptop. He kept whispering "fascinating" and "extraordinary."

Arms crossed, Ivy simply glared at Will. Every time he laughed along with her dad, her eyes narrowed.

Finally, she said, "This movie blows. Let's go play Bloody Mina."

"What's that?" Will asked.

"Local ghost story about a girl who died horribly. They say if you go into a dark room and say 'Bloody Mina' into a mirror three times, her ghost will appear to violently murder you."

"Well, that's bleak," Mr. Cross noted.

"In any other location, I would label this an urban legend, but in East Emerson it is probably true, just like all the other—" Linus started.

Ivy interrupted by swatting her brother.

"What?" Mr. Cross laughed. "Don't hush for my sake. I think ghost stories are cool. They're not real, so it's fun to let them scare you."

"Not real," Ivy said. "Right."

Mr. Cross and Will were laughing uncontrollably at the movie again. Ivy wasn't. She rolled her eyes and squeezed her hands into fists. "This movie sucks."

"No, it doesn't," Will replied. "I like it."

"How about I make some popcorn?" Mr. Cross asked.

"That'd be great!" Will said.

"Be right back."

As soon as Mr. Cross disappeared into the kitchen, Ivy pinched Will. "Why are you sucking up to my dad? We have more important things to be doing—like saving East Emerson from werewolves."

Will shook his furry face. "We've been working our tails off, and what have we got for it? Having to skip school so our gym teacher doesn't murder us. If Dina Iris and Oracle

Jones need our help so bad, let them come help. They expect too much from us. We're just kids. I think we should tell your dad everything. If he knew about the monsters, maybe he could help us."

"No way," Ivy said.

"I am afraid I concur with my sibling on this point," Linus agreed. "As children, our minds are more malleable, our perceptions flexible. However, for adults, a revelation regarding the existence of the supernatural? It could be devastating. I do not think we should risk it."

"Why not give him a chance?" Will asked. "Let's tell him."

"Go tell your own dad," Ivy snapped.

Will felt his whole body tighten. He wanted to scream at Ivy, "*I would if my dad would call me back!*" But he didn't. Instead, he crossed his arms, gritted his teeth until his jaw ached, and glared at Ivy.

Ivy glared right back.

"What's your problem?" Will snapped.

"What's *your* problem?" she snapped back.

Both of them were boiling with rage, but neither were 100 percent certain why.

Sensitive Reader, sometimes this happens between even the best of friends. They get sad or mad or jealous because of a simple misunderstanding. Such feelings are easily resolved if both parties are able to express their emotions through clear and concise communication. However, if they do not explain—or if they are not sure how to explain their complicated feelings—this often leads to an aggravating argument or a ferocious fight. In these situations, I find the best policy is to immediately apologize. An apology can save a friendship. It can also save you from a deadly curse put on you by an evil enchantress in possession of the Egyptian *Book of the Dead* in nineteenth-century London. (Trust me on this one.)

But before Will or Ivy could communicate or try to resolve their hurt feelings, there was a quiet knock and an envelope slid under the front door.

Linus hopped off the couch. He looked out the windows, but saw no one. He picked up the letter. "It's addressed to the three of us. And it is in code. Of course it is."

[A-W]

Edih dfyojq di pslh.

Yic tij'd pwbs di vs hwaje oj dpoe twjqsfice qwks.

Or yic mssh qiojq,

O aij'd vs wvls di hfidsud yic...wqwoj.

Wjt yic aoll kied usfdwojly TOS.

—W

Will pulled out Pamiver's golden pyramid. He twisted it until *A* was in the same column as *W*. Quickly, he translated it while the sounds of popping corn kernels came from the kitchen.

"Butter and salt?" Mr. Cross asked.

"Sure!" Will said.

Ivy rolled her eyes. "Seriously?"

Will returned to decoding the letter. "It's a warning. They want us to stop, that they won't be able to save us again?"

"*Again?*" Ivy realized who it was from. "It's from the gray-skinned man, isn't it? The bearded dude who saved us from the spiders and from Ozzie?"

"But he works for her," Will said. "Whose side is he really on then?"

"Let us table that conversation for now," Linus whispered. "I wanted to tell you about something I found in my research. Wolfsbane, also known as monkshood and *Aconitum*, is a perennial plant with purple petals native to mountainous regions. It is extremely poisonous to humans and deadly to werewolves."

"We already knew that part," Ivy said. "Oracle told us."

"Yes, but not in such detail," Linus said. "It is vitally important for me to find a sampling of the plant to study.

Perhaps I could concoct some derivative elixir to create a cure, or at least something to fend off Ewflower."

"Where do we find it?" Will asked. "Pharmacy? Grocery store? Maybe a farmers market?"

"Therein lies the complication," Linus said. "The strain of wolfsbane referred to here is nearly extinct, thus a difficult plant to track down."

"Thanks for nothing then," Ivy grumbled.

Will snapped, "Ivy, chill out. Linus is doing his best. It wouldn't kill you to be nice to him. Or your dad, for that matter. You should be grateful for a father who wants to stick around. Stop being a jerk."

Ivy exploded. "I'm not a jerk! *You're* the jerk! And this is *my* family. I can talk to them however I want."

Slowly, Mr. Cross reentered the room with two massive bowls of freshly popped popcorn. "Is everything okay? Did I miss something?"

"Only Will trying to *steal my life!*" Ivy shouted.

"What are you talking about?!" Will snapped.

"First you try to be best friends with *my* brother, and now you're obsessed with *my* dad. They're mine, okay?" Ivy's face turned beet red, and her hands squeezed so hard into fists, her knuckles turned white.

Mr. Cross put down the bowls and in a gentle voice said, "Ivy, I'm going to need you to take a deep breath. How about all of us do it? Inhale. Now repeat after me, *I am calm, I am collected, I am among friends*…"

But Ivy refused to breathe. Instead, she shouted at Will, "I don't see any friends here. Get out of my house! GET! OUT!"

"Ivy, you're being rude," Mr. Cross said. "Apologize this instant."

"NO! I want him out of my house! OUT OUT *OUT*!"

"Fine!" Will got up and stormed out. His stomach was in knots before he even got to the other side of the street. It felt like he'd just lost his only friends—like his father was leaving all over again. His face felt hot and he wanted to hit something. He kicked his mailbox. It didn't hurt the mailbox, Dear Reader. It only hurt Will's foot.

Linus shouted after him, "Will! Will, wait."

"Why? Are *you* going to yell at me too?"

"Of course not. I wanted to apologize. My sister's behavior was unfounded and inappropriate. Sometimes, she gets a bit…defensive."

"Yeah, I noticed," Will growled.

"And you? You seem upset as well. Is something bothering you?"

"Like you care."

"I do, or I wouldn't have asked," Linus said quietly.

Will wanted to tell Linus about his dad. But even the thought of Dad's unreturned calls made Will feel like he was on fire. He felt…furious. Not with Linus, but with the world. With his parents for divorcing. With his dad for disappearing. For being turned into a werewolf. Suddenly, it felt like everyone was an enemy. Before he knew it, Will was shouting at Linus: "You know what, it's none of your business!"

Linus took a step back, his eyes full of hurt. "Perhaps… perhaps we should put the investigation on hold for a few days," Linus suggested. "Give Ivy—and you—some time to cool off."

"Great idea," Will said. "Or maybe we should just never speak again."

Then he stormed inside his house and slammed his front door as hard as he could.

chapter 7
the name on the tombstone

✳

When it came to holidays, Thanksgiving had always been Will's favorite. Sure, Halloween was fun for dressing up in costume, and Christmas was great because he got presents, but it was "Turkey Day"—as his dad called it—that Will looked forward to all year long. It was a Hunter family tradition for the men to cook for the women. And that meant it was up to Will and his father to create a feast.

When he was five, he helped his dad make the mashed potatoes—only he put in too much cream and butter and it turned into potato soup. When he was eight, he made green bean casserole—except he used cream of tomato instead of cream of mushroom, and the final presentation looked like a reindeer had thrown up. Two years back, Will and Dad were so busy focusing on the side dishes, they forgot to set a timer—and the turkey came out blacker than a burned grilled cheese. Every Thanksgiving had been a mess, but every disaster turned into laughter and a story for the next year.

But this year, Will thought, no one was going to be laughing.

What was Thanksgiving without Dad?

Will picked up the phone and dialed his father's number. It rang six times, then went to voice mail. "Dad, it's me. Will. Again. Um… Thanksgiving is almost here and it made me think about last year, how we finally made everything perfect—till I dropped the marshmallow yams. And you laughed so hard wine came out your nose…"

The memory made Will smile. It also made him want to cry. He didn't know what else to say. He hated leaving these voice mails. He wanted to talk with his dad, *to* him. Where was he? Was he busy with a new job? A new family? Will knew that his dad had left Brooklyn when Will and his mom left, that he'd taken a new job in California. But a different time zone was no excuse not to return his calls.

Will remembered he was still leaving a voice mail. So he finished: "…okay, well…call me. Bye."

After he hung up, Will had to resist the urge to throw the phone at the wall. Why wasn't Dad calling him back?

The phone rang.

Will's heart swelled as he answered. "Dad?"

"Not quite," said Linus on the other end of the line.

It felt like Will's heart fell out of his chest and onto the floor. "What do you want?"

"I am calling because it has been over a week since your quarrel with Ivy. I am still unclear as to *why* you two are fighting, or *what* you are fighting about—but we need to return to our investigation. Time is of the essence. The full moon is only two weeks away, and I suspect you are tired of shampooing your entire body."

"Whenever Ivy is ready to apologize, I'm ready to listen," Will said.

A loud *"HAH!"* sounded on the other end of the line. Ivy's voice called out from the background, "No way! Tell Will that *he* needs to say sorry *first*. He started this!"

"Am I on speakerphone?" Will snapped.

"This is ridiculous," Linus said to them both.

"Tell him I am not apologizing until he does!" Ivy shouted.

After a sigh, Linus said, "My sister declines the role of

first apology. Will, can you please do it, so we can move forward?"

"No," Will said.

As you may or may not know, Dear Reader, people are stubborn. Born out of pride, being stubborn is a ridiculous attribute in humans—and one, I might add, that is rarely helpful. If only my father had swallowed his pride all those centuries ago, we might have enjoyed a loving and healthy relationship where he attended my soccer matches or watched me learn to stake vampires with one hand tied behind my back. Instead, he chose to hold on to his foolish and old-fashioned notions that children should not be monsters. What he never seemed to grasp was that some children can't help but be monsters, and being a monster isn't necessarily bad in and of itself. It's what we do with our monstrousness that counts.

Both Will and Ivy refused to apologize first. After a deeper, heavier sigh, Linus said, "I suppose we remain at a standoff."

"Guess so," Will said.

Linus whispered into the phone. "Please, Will. I beg of you. Be the bigger person. Apologize so we can find the wolfsbane, defeat Ewflower, and turn you back into a normal boy. Certainly, you cannot live your life in fear of becoming a full-fledged wolf on the full moon of every month."

Will wanted to. But when he thought about Ivy and the way she treated her father…he got mad all over again. "I just can't. Talk to you later, Linus."

Will hung up.

💀💀💀

That night, Will dreamed of running down a long hallway, chasing after his dad. Each time he was about to catch up, his father disappeared through another door. No matter how fast he ran, he could never get to him.

As he shook himself awake, the cold night air tickled his fur. He reached for his blanket, but found nothing. He could hear the churn of the sea in the distance and smell the salt on the air, but it wasn't until he opened his eyes that he found himself standing outside in the darkness. Shadows of crosses and rectangles with curved tops lay scattered about under the light of the crescent moon.

"Not again," he whispered.

He was standing in the middle of the Emerson Cemetery. In his pajamas. For the second time in two months.

He ducked behind a tombstone. Last time he found

himself in the cemetery in the dead of night, it was filled with Ozzie and her wicked Thirteen. But as his heartbeat slowed, Will realized he didn't hear chanting, and there was no sign of a bonfire. Instead, he saw a familiar and friendly soft glow. The fox appeared, rubbing her cheek against his leg.

"Dina Iris? Did you call me here?"

"In a world full of aggressions, I know you have many questions," the fox said. *"I called you here because you asked; I called you here to discuss the past."*

She waved Will after her with a paw, then ran in the other direction. Will raced to follow her, dodging dead tree branches reaching out over the graves. As they weaved through the yard, the stones grew older and more decrepit. The dates went backward, from the 2000s to the 1900s and finally to the late 1800s.

The fox slowed to a trot and stopped in front of a tombstone. Will tried to catch his breath as he arrived. "Why…" he wheezed, "…are you…making me…chase you?"

"Truth is rarely earned so easily. One must work to gain what is not free."

"Do you always have to speak in riddles?"

"My words are bound by a higher law, making it

hard to tell you all I saw. But listen close, listen today, for this is what I'm allowed to say: You and I are tied to this town, as surely as a queen and crown. Our blood goes back generations from long ago, just as the witch and warlock, our deadliest foe."

"I'm sorry, but I don't understand," Will stammered. "Can't you be more clear?"

"As clear as night turned into day, my light should guide you to look this way." The fox's tail brushed against the gravestone behind her. It read:

Here lies
WILLIAM JOHN HUNTER
1846–1870

Will fell backward. He scrambled away, as though he could escape his name that was on the burial marker. He swallowed a scream.

"Is that… Is that me? Is that my grave?!"

The fox shook her head. "No."

"Right. I knew that," Will whispered, trying to calm his racing heart. "My full name is Guillermo Benjamin Hunter, *not* William John. So obviously that's not me."

"*Yet it is your blood, from years of yester, for this is the grave of your ancestor.*"

"A relative?" Will asked, shocked. "How did I not know that?"

"*Time is long, the world is wide, and old truths are easy to hide. What you miss or cannot find, are also the things that truly bind.*"

"Why are you showing me this?"

"*You asked how you could see world and spirits both, now you know 'tis a family's oath. The first Will Hunter was a man of good. He saved this town when no one could. Then he swore for days future and past'ing, his family would help destroy evil everlasting.*"

Will's head swam with too many questions. "Are you saying that's how I see the supernatural? Because my ancestor lived here? That this other Will Hunter helped East Emerson because of a family oath?"

"*Responsibilities are heavy to carry—especially when promised to fight the scary.*"

"I'm really beginning to hate your rhymes," Will whispered. He kneeled next to the tombstone and traced the letters with his finger. "So my dad's dad's dad's dad's dad or something like that lived here in East Emerson? Does that mean—"

Will didn't get to finish his thought as Dina Iris stood, her ears alert. *"Danger approaches from the east; best pretend not to know her in the least. Mind the violence she will sow; instead pretend the witch you do not know."*

"Wait, what?!" Will whispered.

"Some last advice before I go, listen fast, digest it slow: swallow all of your foolish pride, for in your friends you must confide." Then the fox shifted into a worm, wiggled into the dirt, and disappeared.

At the other end of the graveyard, a thick fog rolled forward, in step with a sinister silhouette.

Will ducked, trying to shrink behind the old gravestone, hissing to himself: "I'm alone—barefoot—in the cemetery—in the middle of the night—with danger nearby—again! Thanks for *nothing*, Dina Iris."

As soon as the mysterious figure passed, Will crept in the other direction. He hid from tombstone to mausoleum, from fountain to statue. He was almost out of the cemetery—when he crashed into the tall woman. He looked up slowly. He couldn't believe his lack of luck.

It was Ozzie.

The night air was frigid, but not nearly as cold as the menacing stare of the witch who'd threatened his life on Halloween. Her pale features might have been beautiful if they weren't so terrifying. It was strange to think she was centuries old, when she looked like she was barely twenty. She wore her signature long cloak, hiding her hands until she moved her tattooed arm to her hip, purposely flashing the glimmer of a dagger.

Will desperately tried to ignore the pounding in his heart and the voice in his head screaming "*Run!*" The only way he could survive this was to do as Dina Iris had said: pretend not to know her. Will took a deep breath, then forced a smile.

"Oops! Pardon me!" Will chuckled. "Wasn't watching where I was going. I didn't expect to run into anybody here. Funny, isn't it?"

The witch spun her fingers in a circle, chanting, "*Hturt eht kaeps.*" The purple spell shimmered, flowing from her fingers into Will's throat.

"Yes, it certainly is *funny*," the witch sneered, her eyes locked on Will, "that a boy of your age, at this hour, would be here, while the rest of the town slumbers. Even more *funny*, given our past meeting. Now that I've spelled you, you can only speak the truth. So tell me, what are you doing here?"

Will's mind raced. If he told her the truth, she would…

Gulp.

He reinforced his smile. "Why wouldn't I speak the truth? Of course I'll speak the truth. And you say we met? When? Are you sure? I'm sure I'd remember someone as tall as you. And you have purple hair. Did you know that?" The truth was trying to force its way up, to spill out onto his tongue, but Will kept dancing around it by asking questions or stating facts. "Are you new to town? I am. I'm new here. I moved here last month. From Brooklyn. Ever been?"

"A long time ago," she said, her eyes studying him. "Why are you here, boy? In the middle of the night?"

"Oh, well, I guess I couldn't sleep. So I came out here. I don't live that far. This place is, uh…pretty spooky, right?"

"Are you alone?"

"Of course I'm alone," Will said, grateful that the fox had fled. Only, his mouth kept talking. "Well, except that I have family here."

"Where?" Ozzie demanded, pulling the blade from her belt.

Will panicked. He couldn't show her his ancestor's name.

Ozzie was centuries old… What if she knew him? What if they were enemies? But the spell insisted he tell the truth.

Instead of speaking, he pointed to a nearby grave, which simply said:

TO MY LOVING FATHER,
R.I.P.

Ozzie asked, "You lost your father?"

"Yes." It wasn't a lie. Will *had* lost his father. Dad wasn't dead, but he'd certainly disappeared after the divorce.

Ozzie paused, gazing at the grave. "I am…sorry for your loss."

Will stared at the witch as she gazed off into the distance. He'd always thought of her as pure evil. But was she actually being…nice?

She asked, "Do you miss him?"

"Every day." Will didn't want to say more, but the truth pushed its way out of his throat. "I mostly miss the little things. How he made me laugh, how I could tell him anything, how he made me feel safe…"

The words seemed to disarm Ozzie. She returned the blade to her belt. She walked. Entranced, Will followed. "I lost someone too," she said. "He was my sun and my moon and my stars. He was my whole world."

"A parent?" Will asked. "A child?"

"A lover," the witch said. "He was one of the most powerful men on the planet. He would have been a god if not for…" Her voice trailed off.

"Is he buried here?"

"In a matter of speaking," she whispered.

"Is that why you came here tonight? To talk to him? I do that too, try to talk to my dad still…" Will said, unable to stop his own words. He thought fast, thinking of all the voice mails he'd left. "My dad isn't here, though, not physically. I know that. But I still talk to him, as if he's in the same room, hoping he'll listen, hoping he'll talk back to me. Hoping that he'll return to me. But he doesn't. It's like he's forgotten me."

"The dead do not forget," Ozzie said. "Our loved ones wait for us to join them—or bring them back."

"Bring them back?" Will asked.

Ozzie's eyes glowed crimson in the night. She stopped at the edge of the unmarked well, the gaping black hole in the field behind the cemetery, where Will and Ivy had come not so long ago. The witch stared into the mass of black. Will heard—even felt—the sound of the echoing heartbeat coming up from below.

Buh-bum. Buh-bum. Buh-bum.

The witch raised her hand. It began to crackle with

emerald electricity. *"Edoc ni sdrow ym etirw, enots hguorht nrub."* She blasted a ray of energy as bright as the sun, scoring through the rock wall until it left a series of numbers:

08·05·18·05 12·09·05·19
19·09·13·15·14 03·18·15·23·12·05·25 02·09·19·
08·15·16.
02·18·09·14·07 25·15·21·18 04·15·07·19, 05·23·
06·12·15·23·05·18.
02·18·09·14·07 20·08·05·13 08·05·18·05, 01·
14·04 <u>04·09·07</u>.

"What is that?" Will asked.

"A message for someone," Ozzie answered. "But yes… I do come here, like you, to speak to the dead. To tell him I miss him. That my life is less without him…"

There wasn't enough moonlight to be sure, but Will thought he could see a tear on the witch's cheek.

"I wish I could make this…this *hurt* go away," she whispered.

"I know," Will said softly. "One day my dad was part of my everyday life. The next he…he was just…gone. I couldn't see him, or spend time with him, or hear his voice. Like I was a sailboat on the ocean—and the wind vanished. I stopped moving. I felt… I *feel* so alone. All the time. Sometimes I worry it'll last forever."

"So you do understand," Ozzie said. She stole a red rose from a nearby grave and held it out over the well. The fresh red petals began to wither and wilt, blackening, as if some dark force from below were draining them of life. Ozzie tossed the flower into the gaping maw. It disintegrated into dust before it had fallen more than a few feet.

"I miss my Simon. Each and every single day. I hate it," she seethed. "It makes me feel…pathetic and weak…that I cannot move past this pain."

"I know the feeling," Will whispered, biting his lip before he could say, *That's why I call my dad everyday still— even though he never calls me back.* "Don't be too hard on yourself. It's not pathetic. The heart wants what it wants."

Ozzie almost smiled. "Sound advice, child."

Will wondered for a moment if this was the same villain behind the Thirteen, behind all of the terrible things happening in East Emerson. As if in answer, quicker than a crow, Ozzie's hand seized his throat. She began to squeeze. The kindness in her face twisted into something darker.

"The pain is too unbearable, though. That is why I must do everything in my power to make it stop—even if that means crushing this town beneath my heel. Sometimes, the only way to save yourself is to destroy everything else."

Will gasped for air.

"You might think me cruel, boy. But if I crushed your windpipe now, I would save you from the nightmare to come. Trust me, leaving you alive is no mercy. By bringing back Simon, I will unleash untold horrors on this world. Are you certain you want to live, child?"

"Y-yes…" Will's voice cracked.

The witch's eyes searched Will's face for a different answer. He struggled to pry her fingers from his neck, as though he could match her strength.

He couldn't.

He was suffocating.

"As you wish." Ozzie released Will.

He collapsed to the ground, choking for air.

The fog thickened, flowing around the witch, swallowing her completely. But her disembodied voice called back, "Do not spend much time mourning the departed, child—for the dead will rise soon enough."

Chapter 8
Flowers for a Funeral

✳

Will walked downstairs, quickly buttoning his polo shirt all the way up to cover the bruises on his neck. He didn't think the town curse would hide those from his mom. As he sat down to breakfast, he noticed Mom was unusually quiet. She held uneaten toast in her hand, staring off into the distance.

"Mom…are you okay?"

"Oh, Will." She hugged her son. "I am now. But the most frightening thing happened last night. When I got to my car after my shift ended, there was a pack of wild dogs waiting for me. They started chasing me. I was so scared, I dropped my keys. I barely made it back inside the hospital."

Will felt a hard knot form in his throat. "Did they hurt you?"

"No, thank goodness. I'm just glad I made it away safely."

"Me too," Will said, guilt weighing in his stomach like

an anchor. If he and his friends had already solved the mystery behind the werewolves and Ozzie's evil plans, his mom could've avoided such a fright.

"The police are saying there's been a large amount of wild dog activity. Wolves, coyotes, strays, that kind of thing," Mom started. "Tons of people have called the hospital about bites, but very few have come in. The few that have, well—this is the odd part—their bites were already healed up and scarred over as if they'd been bitten months ago."

"That is odd," Will agreed. He pulled up his sock, so Mom didn't see his scar. But what he was thinking was, *Odd for the rest of the world, but normal for East Emerson.*

Mom shook her head, as if trying to forget the terrible experience. "How was your night?"

Will winced. "My night?" He wondered if Mom knew he'd been in a cemetery after midnight again. "Um, I slept fine."

"Good. I'm glad you're feeling better. But please, do me a favor: don't travel alone, don't go out after the sun goes down, and if you see wild dogs—run."

Dear Reader, Ms. Vásquez offers sound advice. I would recommend the same. There is always safety in numbers, and no good occurs after dark. And wild dogs? Well, wild *anything* is something to avoid, be them devil dogs, dog-gish devils, or terrible teenagers.

Mom took a deep breath and ate her toast. She tried to force a smile, but Will saw her face fall as she noticed a pile of unpaid bills on the table.

Will breathed a sigh of relief—not about the bills, mind you, but about his mom not knowing he'd been out again. She had enough on her plate without another argument with her son about saving a town from supernatural things she couldn't see. Will now had a clue to why he *could* see the supernatural. But he wanted to know more. "Hey, Mom. Do I have ancestors here in East Emerson?"

Mom stopped looking at the bills to give her son her full attention. "Well, that's a very specific question that came out of nowhere."

"Oh…yeah…it's for a school project."

"Hmm. Well, you definitely don't from my side of the family. My parents are from Mexico, same with their parents and their parents before that. But maybe on your dad's side? Now that I think about it, I recall your dad mentioning a grand-father who lived in Salem, which isn't far from here. That can't be a coincidence. You should call your father and—"

Will stopped eating. Slowly, he pushed the cereal bowl away.

Mom reached out, putting her hand on Will's. "He hasn't called you back, has he?"

Will shook his head. "I don't get it. I've called, like, a hundred times. Did I... Did I do something wrong?"

"No, of course not," Mom said. "The divorce had absolutely nothing to do with you. Your father and I had grown apart. He still loves you. You're his only son. With his move and his new job, maybe he's just...busy."

"Too busy to call? Or even text? It takes, like, two seconds."

"I know. And I'm not defending him. He should call. There's no excuse in my opinion. If the situation were reversed and you were living with him, I'd be calling you every day. Probably three or four times a day. You'd be sick of hearing from me." His mom tried to smile.

Will smiled back. "I'd never be sick of you, Mom."

Ms. Vásquez wrapped her arm around her son. "Whatever the reason your father isn't calling you back, do *not* take it personally. *You* have done nothing wrong. Understand me?"

Will shrugged. "It's hard not to take it personally. Especially with Turkey Day coming up…"

"I know," she said, squeezing him again. "Holidays are about traditions. Not just old ones, like you and your dad cooking, but about making new ones. So this year, let's make some new traditions—with your friends. Mr. Cross invited us to have Friends-Giving with his family. I told him yes. Is that okay?"

Will had never had Thanksgiving with anyone but family. The idea of spending it without Dad was…upsetting. But spending it with friends?

"That sounds really fun, Mom." Will hugged her again, hugged Fitz for good measure, and grabbed his backpack. When she wasn't looking, he also slipped a raw onion into his mom's purse, just in case any more wolves showed up.

"Ivy! Linus! Wait up!" Will called from across the street. He jogged to catch up to them. "I just heard we're spending Thanksgiving together. I'm stoked! You'll have to tell me what your favorite dishes are, because I love to cook! But before that, I have to tell you about last night—"

"Linus, could you please tell Will that I am *not* speaking to him," Ivy said to Linus, pretending not to see Will.

"Wait, seriously?" Will asked. With everything happening, he'd forgotten that he and Ivy had fought. "You need to let that go. We have bigger monsters to fry."

"Linus, could you please tell Will that no, I will not let it go. Not until he says he's sorry."

"I am *not* apologizing," Will growled.

"Linus, could you please tell Will to grow up?"

"Linus, could you please tell Ivy that she's going to want to hear what I have to say?"

"I am not a telephone!" Linus shouted. "The two of you are being childish and immature, and I will not be the middleman here. Speak to one another already!"

"Never mind then!" Will snapped, his anger bubbling up again. "I was all happy to find out that we were spending Thanksgiving together. But maybe I'll just tell my mom I don't want to now."

"That's for the best," Ivy snorted. "My Korean corn bread is to die for, and you don't deserve to taste it."

"Yeah, well, then you'll never know the bliss of my galletas de suero, my chorizo stuffing, or my roasted-pumpkin guacamole!" Will shouted back. "And I won't share with you jerks how last night *Dina Iris* summoned me to the cemetery to show me *my ancestor's grave*, and how I spoke to *Ozzie* about how she's going to bring *Simon back from the dead*."

"Wait, what?!" Ivy and Linus yipped at the same time. "Tell us everything!"

"No," Will snapped. Then he turned around and stormed

off, his face flushed red, burning with anger—even though he wasn't sure what he and Ivy were even arguing about anymore.

☠☠☠

Will regretted his behavior immediately after walking away toward school. He didn't know why he kept getting so angry with his friends when he knew he was actually angry about his dad. What had Dina Iris said the night before? About swallowing his pride and confiding in his friends? But how could he tell them without looking stupid?

As Will approached his school, he saw that the whole front had been vandalized. Spray-painted in giant letters was a series of numbers:

[X = 3]

25-13-10 11-26-17-17 18-20-20-19 14-24 08-20-18-
14-19-12 11-06-24-25...
23-10-18-10-18-07-10-23 25-20 07-14-25-10 04-
20-26-23 11-23-14-10-19-09-24.

He took out Ewflower's golden pyramid and noticed it was built just like Pamiver's. He found the release and clicked it, twisting until the *X* matched up with the number 3.

"Another secret message," Will whispered.

Will quickly realized today was going to be more bizarre than usual. And that's saying something, considering the school had a pukwudgie principal, a naiad nurse, and an Arikura-no-baba adviser.

Inside, the hallways were packed with werewolves—students and faculty alike—fur-faced, pointy-eared, black-eyed, and noses sniffing nonstop. Students barked, teachers chased their own tails, and more than a few were peeing in random corners. The janitor took one look, threw down his mop, and shouted, "*I quit!!*"

"Oh, no," Will whispered, "so many people have been bitten."

"*Achoo!* Isn't it *achoo!* just awful?" Mr. Villalobos asked. He blew his nose into a tissue. "All of this *achoo!* wolf dander makes my allergies go crazy."

"How are you allergic to yourself?" Will asked.

"Bad genes, I guess," the math teacher said. "Lycanthropy *and* allergies to pets runs in my family. But at least I was born this way. I wasn't *turned* against my will by that rude and abominable Coach Ewflower. She doesn't even ask people for consent first—she just bites them, or has her minions do it. It's deplorable behavior and gives the wolf community a bad name."

Will looked wide-eyed at his teacher. "Wow. That was honest."

The math teacher shrugged. "It's not like you're going

to remember anyways. The town curse will make you forget any second."

"Right…" Will said. Then he put on his best fake-confused face and added, "Forget what?"

"Exactly," the math teacher said, walking away.

As Will turned the corner, he saw Coach Ewflower herself approaching a human colleague. "Mrs. Raleigh, could I speak with you for just a moment?" Ewflower escorted her into the teacher's lounge.

As soon as the door closed, Will ran over. He lifted himself up onto the tips of his shoes and stole a glance through the small window. Before he could do anything, Ewflower bit Mrs. Raleigh.

"Ow! Why would you do that?!" the teacher cried, gripping her arm.

"Because I want you to be part of my pack," Coach Ewflower said, wiping the blood from her mouth. "As I am your Alpha, you'll do anything I tell you. By the end of the day, I want you to have bitten five more people."

"I'll do…no such…" Mrs. Raleigh stuttered. Already, she was starting to lose her willpower as her face grew furry and her eyes turned black and entranced. She bowed her head. "What else can I do for you, my Alpha?"

"Tonight, at midnight, meet me at the cemetery—and bring a shovel," Ewflower sneered. "Now go about your day. Behave normally, and forget we had this conversation."

"Yes, ma'am."

Will jumped to the side of the door as the art teacher came out. Mrs. Raleigh walked down the hall, her fresh bite healing miraculously. She was completely mind-controlled in mere seconds. Will felt lucky to have Oracle Jones and her witch brew to keep him safe from that.

When the door shut, Will heard more talking.

"Half of the townspeople are under my control now," Ewflower said. "Is that enough?"

"No. I want the *entire* town turned," said another. Will knew the raspy voice. It was Ozzie. He peeked back through the window. The witch leaned against the far wall, petting Faust who lay sleeping in her arm. "All of you dogs will do my bidding."

"We *aren't* dogs," Ewflower growled. "We are wolves."

"Swallow your ridiculous pride," Ozzie sneered. "You've been a werewolf for less than a month. You're only an Alpha because I turned you into one and gave you the power to take a foothold in this town. But remember: *you* work for *me*—if I want you to play fetch, you'll play fetch. If I want you to dig holes, you'll dig holes. Am I clear?"

"Crystal clear," Ewflower seethed. "But when we're done excavating the tunnels—once we find Simon's bones beneath the cave-in—we'll be free to go, as you promised?"

"We'll see," Ozzie said. "I'll let you know."

"That wasn't the deal!" Ewflower roared.

"The deal has changed—"

Will slipped, falling against the door with a loud *THUD!*

"What was that?" Coach Ewflower asked.

Will scrambled to get up, then ran down the hall. He raced into a bathroom, flung himself into a stall, and hid there. Trying, and failing, to catch his breath, he hoped and prayed Ozzie wouldn't follow him. He waited a long time before he decided it was safe to go to class.

When he stepped out of the stall, he looked at himself in the mirror. Under his fur, he was pale, and his hands were shaking. He knew Ozzie wanted an army, but the whole town? That meant Will's mom, and Mr. Cross, and everyone else they knew. And Ewflower was the Alpha, forcing the newly turned wolves to dig Simon's bones out of the tunnels below?

He'd heard all he needed to hear. He didn't have time

to act like a brat anymore. He had to tell Ivy and Linus everything. They had to stop this before things got worse.

☠☠☠

When the lunch bell rang, Will ran out of his classroom and through the halls like someone fleeing a tidal wave. He raced into the cafeteria and toward Ivy. "We have to talk. Where's Linus?"

"Right here," Linus said, walking up from behind. "Have either of you observed that our educational institution smells of dog urine?"

"Yup. The boy werewolves are marking their territory between classes," Ivy said, shuddering. "Someone even peed on my locker."

"No more jokes!" Will roared. "Ozzie wants Ewflower to turn the entire town into werewolves! And I know why…" Will told them everything: about Dina Iris and the grave with Will's ancestor, about Ozzie and her plan to resurrect Simon, about Ewflower being ordered to turn the entire town into werewolves…

"Diabolical," Linus said. "If the coach only bites five people today, then commands those five wolves to bite five more, that's already twenty-five werewolves. If those five do the same, and their five follow suit—" Linus was doing the math in his head. "We're going to have a pyramid epidemic on our hands. The rest of the town will be turned in a matter of days."

"So what do we do?" Will asked.

Ivy gently pulled down Will's collar. Purple bruises showed where Ozzie had choked him. Her face hardened. "We need to leave town."

"I'm serious," Will said.

"So am I," Ivy said. "I'd love to save East Emerson, but this is too much, even for us."

Linus adjusted his glasses. "We need a plan."

"Screw a plan! We need to get our families packed up and ditch this place!" Ivy snapped. "I don't want the people I love getting hurt!"

Linus slammed his hands down on the table. "Ivy, shut up and listen to me for once!" Surprisingly, Ivy did as her brother commanded. "Look, even if we could talk our parents into leaving—which I highly doubt we can—what about the rest of the population? They'd be left to fall victim to Ozzie's dreadful plan. Could you really live with yourself if you abandoned all the innocents of East Emerson?"

"To save my family? Heck yeah." Ivy crossed her arms. Then she hesitated. "Maybe. I mean, I don't know. I guess not."

"And you, Will?"

"No. We need to stay and fight."

"Exactly. And for that, we need a plan. Let us consider what we know.

"Last month, Ozzie had Pamiver building an army of vampire animals, to keep the citizens sleepy and confused and blood-drained. We thwarted that plan. Now she is building an army of werewolves—to use as workers to dig up Simon in the tunnels below East Emerson.

"Then, based on what Will has told us, she'll bring Simon back from the dead. And things will go from bad to worse—"

"The end of days," Ivy finished.

"As for a plan, I suggest this: after school, we return the *Lost Things* book to Ms. Delphyne. Maybe she has located helpful information about undoing the effects of a wolfen state. In that case, we can change everyone back. If not, at the very least, perhaps she can help us formulate a strategy to derail Ozzie's plan," Linus said.

He continued, "Until the end of school, we need to adhere to our regular class schedules. If we cut class, we could get detention. And I refuse to let my record be marred just because some ancient witch is trying to destroy my town. Is everyone on the same page?"

Will and Ivy nodded. They were both impressed with Linus's forceful leadership.

"Good. Now eat your lunch. You'll need your strength. Ivy, rub another raw onion on your neck, just to be safe. I'll do the same. For the rest of the day, we need to *not* get bit."

"Good call, little brother," Ivy said.

"Thank you," Linus said, pushing his glasses up his nose. "It is about time someone started recognizing the might of my mind."

💀💀💀

When the three friends arrived at the library, a few senior citizens were browsing books or napping by the newspapers. Linus fast walked over to the lamia and opened his backpack so she could see the book.

She wrapped her arms around Linus. "You found it!"

Linus blushed.

The snake-tailed librarian scanned the room, as if expecting spies. She whispered, "Let's go to my office."

Will and Ivy followed and locked the door behind them. Linus handed the book to Ms. Delphyne, and her eyes watered while she hugged it, as if a missing child had been returned. "How can I ever repay you?"

"Did you have a chance to research any potential cures or treatments against werewolfism?" Will asked.

"I did," Ms. Delphyne said, pulling out her laptop and showing the trio her work. "I searched everywhere, from Babylonian texts to medieval literature. Sadly, nothing I found speaks of an ultimate cure—at least not for those *born* into lycanthropy. For those who were 'made by bite,' they can be 'unmade' if the Alpha 'renounces the beast.' I found several accounts where a pack leader commanded his or her tribe to suppress their wolfen natures in order to hide in plain sight and pass for normal."

"So if Ewflower tells her army to stop being werewolves—" Linus whispered.

Dahlia finished, "Then the werewolves would be human again."

"So now we just need to talk Ewflower into doing that?" Ivy snorted. "I don't think that's going to work."

"I suspect you're right," Ms. Delphyne said. "Outside of that, two materials came up again and again: silver and wolfsbane. Because both are lethal in large doses, they are most often used as a defense mechanism. One Arthurian poem in particular seemed to speak of a kind of aid: 'Petal of Wolf's Bane once a day, keeps the wolf at bay or away.'"

"What does that mean?" Will asked.

"I suspect ingesting wolfsbane will either repel were-wolves or keep the wolf within contained. Of course that's pure conjecture," the librarian explained.

Ivy threw up her arms in frustration. "But Linus said wolfsbane is hard to find."

"That is a problem," the librarian noted.

Linus laid his head down on *The History of Lost Things*, moaning, "Where are we going to find wolfsbane?"

The book binding pushed Linus back, opening itself. The pages began to turn on their own again.

"What sorcery is this?" Ms. Delphyne asked.

"I don't know," Linus whispered, "but I think the book is trying to help us. Look." The pages stopped on a spread labeled "Bane of Wolf." It displayed a drawing of the purple-petaled flower and had an entry written in strange symbols.

"It's Runor, an alphabet in runes," Ms. Delphyne noted. "Here, let me translate it for you… 'Before Emer the Red sailed to the new world…before he was a killer of monsters…he was a boy whose home was plagued…by werewolves.'"

The trio exchanged glances as the lamia librarian continued to translate.

"'His mother forged him a sword of silver at the age of eight…and his father taught him the power of the Bane of Wolf, a flower that would protect him… When he set sail, never to return to his birth shores…he took the flower with him, planting it nearby. He would one day take it to his grave.'"

"Nice story," Ivy said, "but that doesn't help us."

"Or does it?" Will whispered. "Listen to this last line. If he took it to his grave, and he died in East Emerson, then maybe…"

Linus rested his hand on the book, asking it, "Where did Emer the Red die?"

Once again, the pages began to turn on their own. They settled on a different entry. Linus said, "It's a journal entry, written by Emer's wife, Artemis."

Ms. Delphyne took the book and translated it: "'Emer's

plan was a success. All of us worked, and fought, together. We could not kill the serpent god, but we could trap it. And so we did. But at great cost. A hundred and twenty of our warriors—men, women, and children—lie dead. My sweet Emer among them…'

"There's a gap on the page, and drops. As if she were crying. Poor woman. Then she continues here: 'Emer always loved a view. I will lay him to rest at the highest peak on this island, so that he can always be sure to watch over it. I will plant seeds around him, so that he will grow and live again, among the flowers of his homeland…'"

"The highest peak in East Emerson is Viking View—" Linus said. "Our parents took us there for a picnic last summer."

"We complained the whole time," Ivy whispered, exchanging a glance with Linus.

"But there were purple flowers there," Linus noted, "under a great tree. It is an extensive hike, but if we leave now, we can get there before the sun goes down."

"Viking's View?" Ms. Delphyne asked. "Just this morning, a university professor—a Dr. Daednu—came in asking after local topography maps, as well as books on botany. He seemed a little anxious about the whole thing. It's too uncanny to be a coincidence."

Will said, "What if Ewflower already studied the book and found out?"

"But Ozzie wants the wolves digging. Why would they go after the wolfsbane?" Linus asked.

Ivy answered, "Ozzie wouldn't, but Ewflower would. Wolfsbane is the only thing that can stop her. She'd want to make sure no one could use it against her."

"If the bad guys know, we better hurry," Will said, "or it's us against the wolves."

chapter 9
race to the grave

＊

"Why are we always riding our bikes to save the day?" Ivy asked, as she pedaled ahead of her brother and Will. The three were struggling to get their bikes up the foothill of Viking's View. "We're the town heroes: we need *speed*— like a car or a truck!"

"And who, pray tell, is going to be our driver?" Linus asked. "We are all minors."

"This is East Emerson," Ivy noted, "we should have jet packs!"

"That'd be cool," Will said. "I'd love to fly."

"No one is talking to you," Ivy said.

"Wait—you're still mad at me?"

"I was never not mad," Ivy noted. "I was just focusing on the mystery at hand."

"Ivy, please, let it go," Linus pleaded.

"I will. As soon as I get that apology."

"I'm sorry…" Will started, "…sorry that you're so rude to your dad when all he's trying to do is be a good parent."

Ivy swerved her bike and rammed into Will's. He nearly crashed, but managed to catch himself. He shouted, "You almost knocked me off the road!!"

"Yes. Yes, I did, dog-face," Ivy growled. "You don't know the first thing about me and the people I care about. So back off!"

Linus stopped his bike between them. He put up his hands. "Might we call a temporary truce? At least until *after* we have found the wolfsbane? We are about to rush into a potential conflict, and I would like my associates to at least appear to be working together. If not for me, then for East Emerson."

"Fine," Ivy moaned.

"Fine," Will groaned.

At the base of the hiking trail, Will looked up. There were no roads going up to the highest point, just a few dirt paths. The grass was straw-colored, dotted with red, orange, and yellow leaves fallen from trees that spotted the hillside. In the distance, he could see the ocean water rolling in waves toward the rocky coast. There was a tiny island with a decrepit lighthouse and a half-sunken tugboat on its shore. A chilling autumn breeze flew in, bringing with it the scent of salt and fish. Will zipped up his jacket.

"We need to get in and out before we are detected," Linus noted. "We are no match for werewolves, especially if we are outnumbered."

"Then we better hurry," Ivy said. She took her brother's giant backpack, strapped it on, and jogged up the hill.

Only a few minutes in, Linus and Will were winded. Linus asked, "Does anyone observe an escalator or an elevator or a ski lift?"

"I wish," said Will.

"Put your back into it, boys," Ivy said, racing up the steep hillside. "We need to get there before the sun sets or we won't be able see a thing."

"I'm not sure that's going to be our problem," Will said, pointing. Black smoke was rising above the top of the mount. "Where there's smoke, there's fire."

"Hurry!"

The trio raced up the hill. By the time they got to the top, Will's and Linus's lungs burned, starving for air. They thought they were going to pass out as Ivy pushed them behind a boulder to hide. Nearby, a giant oak tree shaped like a claw marked the highest point. Its base was surrounded by a lush mass of purple petals. Approaching was Coach Ewflower and a crew of six in firefighter gear—each sporting fur, fangs, and black eyes. With two tank backpacks and a set of flamethrowers, they started to set fire to the lush purple flowers.

"Are those firefighters *starting* a fire?" Ivy asked.

"It is a controlled burn," Linus explained. "Fire control authorities utilize prescribed hazard-reduction burning, where they purposely set fires for forest management to decrease the likelihood of more serious *un*controlled fires. Though in this instance, it appears they are simply here to burn away any vegetation that might be the *Aconitum*."

"In English please," Ivy said.

"They are going to burn the entire area to destroy any wolfsbane that grows here."

"Great," Ivy sneered sarcastically.

Linus pointed. "They are starting on the far side. There's too much to do all at once. When they turn their backs over there, we'll have a moment to grab some. We can hide behind those rocks as we approach and leave. Follow me, and if you see any purple flowers, take them."

The three friends approached carefully and ducked behind the crop of boulders. Will peeked over and saw a small stone tablet with Viking runes carved into it. He whispered, "That must be it, were Artemis buried Emer."

"Save the sightseeing for another time. For now, focus on the flowers," Linus whispered.

When Will noticed a flower within arm's length, he reached out for it. No sooner had he touched the stem than his flesh boiled and blistered, wisps of smoke rising from it.

Will clamped his other hand over his mouth half a second before he screamed out in agony.

"Are you okay?" Ivy whispered.

Will shook his head, tears of pain on his cheeks. He took a few deep breaths, then whispered, "The wolfsbane works as advertised."

Ivy reached into the largest side pocket on Linus's backpack and retrieved the first aid kit. She wrapped Will's still-sizzling hand with white gauze.

"I'm fine," Will said. "Get the flowers."

"No," Ivy said. "I'm taking care of you first."

For some reason, Will was taken aback. Surprised Reader, if you're anything like Will—or most human beings—when you meet someone, you consider them to be one-dimensional. Take Ivy, for instance: many would say she's sporty, selfish, and somewhat snippy. I will not lie—those traits *do* describe her. But that is not all there is to Ivy. Though she does not often show it, she is also loyal and fiercely protective of those she loves, including Will. Sure, she enjoys pestering and pranking and poking fun at her brother, as that's what brothers and sisters do, but she would protect Linus with her own life. And though she was currently furious with Will, she still considered him a friend. A close friend. Maybe even a best friend. (Though of course, she would never admit this out loud.)

Dear Reader, most people are like this: they have obvious behaviors, but they also have characteristics they keep hidden. As a monster, I often see people as they truly are—compassionate, kind, and loving. They do not mean to be cruel when they set me on fire. They do it out of love—not for me, obviously, but for those they are trying to safeguard. Most people will do anything to protect a person in their pack.

As with any rule, there are exceptions. For instance, Will's father not returning his calls. That, and my own parental units. I simply cannot fathom why my own father and mother would bring me into this world only to ignore me. I bet that dog poo on the bottom of their shoe gets more attention from them than I do. Why? I haven't a clue. If you ever find out, do let me know. Back to the adventure…

While Ivy took care of Will, Linus carefully climbed up onto the rocks. He stayed low, crawled forward, and plucked as many flowers as he could, even as the fire inched toward him. He filled his pants pockets, then his jacket pockets, then rushed to grab more, when he was lifted up from behind.

Linus dangled five feet above the ground, held in the air by a firefighter baring sharp werewolf teeth. "Salutations," Linus said. "A fine day for flower picking, is it not?"

"Coach!" the firefighter werewolf called out.

From the other side of the fire and smoke, Ewflower spotted Linus, along with Ivy and Will. She shouted, "Bring them to me."

Linus looked at the firefighter. "As one male to another, I apologize in advance." With all his strength, he kicked the large man right in his—how do I put this delicately?—right between his legs. The firefighter crumbled to the ground as Linus landed on his feet and raced toward his friends. "Run!"

"Did you get enough wolfsbane?" Ivy cried.

"We will have to make do," Linus said. He ushered his sister and neighbor to their feet, and all three of them sprinted down the hill.

"After them!" Coach Ewflower cried out.

The three raced down the hill, skipping over the trails, as fast as deer, careful not to trip or fall. Behind them, Coach Ewflower screamed orders for her crew to move faster. One man tripped and tumbled down like a rock. Another crashed into someone else, knocking them both down.

"Buffoons! All of you!" the coach shouted.

"Almost to the bottom," Ivy said.

"Oh, no. We have company…" Will called out. Two more werewolves waited for them below, standing between them and their bikes.

Will, Ivy, and Linus slowed as they realized they had nowhere to go. Two adults in front, three more coming down from behind, and two were slowly coming up on each side. They were surrounded.

"Dang it, come on." Ivy glared at Will. "Where's your magic fox when we need her?"

"I wish I knew," he said. "Maybe you could use your powers of sarcasm against the werewolves."

"I know you," Ewflower called out as she walked down the hillside toward them. "You three are in my gym class. I'm guessing that you're also the ones who broke into my home, stole the book, and maced me—aren't you?"

"Maybe?" Ivy answered.

"Making an enemy of me wasn't very smart," Ewflower snapped.

"Well, I'm not known for being smart," Ivy said.

"What are your names?"

"Luke, Leia, and Han," Will lied.

"Tweedledee, Tweedledum, and Tweedledumber," Ivy lied.

"Athos, Porthos, and Aramis," Linus also lied. Though Ivy and Will looked at him with questioning eyes. "They're the heroes from *The Three Musketeers*."

Coach Ewflower glared. She locked her eyes on to Will. "You, boy. You've been bitten by one of my wolves. That means you're in my pack and under my control. I command you, tell me your names."

Will felt the strange magical tug of his Alpha. He wanted

to obey. But Oracle Jones's witch brew was stronger. He shook his head. "No."

Ewflower stopped walking, stumped. "Tell me!"

Will resisted with a smile. "I said no."

Ewflower slammed her werewolf arm into a nearby tree. It cracked in half. "Do you see my strength? Don't be a fool. Give up now. I'll turn these two humans and let you all live. But first, give us the flowers."

"You want these?" Ivy asked, grabbing a handful from Linus. She waved them in front of Ewflower, who growled as she leaped back. "Come and take them—if you can."

Linus grabbed the flowers from his jacket pockets, holding them up like two bouquets. Linus and Ivy were back-to-back, with Will on the side, growling. Slowly, the werewolves approached.

"We're trapped," Will said.

"How do we get away?" Ivy asked.

"Use the silver dagger Oracle gave you!" Linus said.

"Um, I kinda left it at home," Ivy admitted. Linus groaned. "I forgot, okay? You know I'm bad at homework."

The wolf circle tightened around the young heroes. Linus swung his flowers like a sword. When the petals slapped a firefighter's hand, he screamed in agony as his skin burst into tiny purple flames. Linus shouted, "Stay away from us."

The coach laughed. "There are more of us than of you. You may hurt us with the wolfsbane, but not before we catch at least one of you. And then—" She smiled, her werewolf teeth glinting in the setting sun.

Will and Ivy felt their confidence drop. The Alpha coach was right. The three of them couldn't hold them off. They were done for.

SLAM!

A giant gray fist punched one of the firefighters in the side of the face, knocking him unconscious before he hit the ground ten feet away. The three friends looked up.

"LEAVE THEM ALONE." The massive gray stranger stood there, fuming. In the fiery dusk light, they could see that his flesh wasn't just gray but had sections of green, gray, and brown skin stitched together like a patchwork quilt. He was thick and muscular, nearly eight feet tall, with fists the size of melons, and a black beard with a red stripe in it.

"WALK AWAY," the stranger said, his voice deeper than a drum. "LEAVE THESE KIDS BE."

"You're one of the Thirteen," Ewflower said. "When I tell Oestre of this—"

He interrupted, "*IF* YOU SURVIVE TO TELL HER OF THIS."

Ewflower laughed, then said to her minions, "Destroy him."

The gray stranger grabbed his first two attackers by their necks—then slammed their heads together. They crumpled to the ground like sleeping dolls. The next werewolf swung, but the stranger ducked, moving more quickly than he should have given his size. He punched the wolf in the chest, sending him tumbling thirty feet away.

The stranger turned to the kids and said, "RUN."

Dear Reader, have you ever heard the adage "Don't look a gift horse in the mouth"? The proverb means "Don't question the value of a gift." In this case, it means Will and friends should *not* take the time to wonder where the gray stranger came from or why he was helping them. Instead, they should simply do as he said and escape with their lives.

Ivy and Linus did just that. They raced the last fifty feet to their bikes and hopped on. Will, on the other hand, did not. Once again, he paused at the patchwork man's side and said, "Who are you? Why are you helping us?"

"BECAUSE IT IS THE RIGHT THING TO DO," he said. "NOW GO."

Will's instinct told him to run. But his heart told him to stay. He couldn't abandon this man to the werewolves—

not after he'd already saved Will's life twice before. Will hesitated, frozen by his own indecision.

"Kill them! Kill them all!" Coach Ewflower shrieked. The last of the werewolves bounded forward, bearing their fangs and claws.

The patchwork man grabbed one of the men by his leg, using him as a whip to smash into three more. Then he tossed him like a rock, battering the others.

"Get up! Attack him again!" the coach cried. "At the same time!"

Her men and women got up, charging again. They clawed and bit, kicked and hit him. He winced from pain, but remained almost unfazed as he used his own body to shield Will. The stranger had two werewolves on every limb and three on his back. He stripped them off one by one, like bark from a tree, so that they landed at Ewflower's feet. The last two people standing were the stranger and Ewflower.

She roared, gnashing her teeth.

"GO NOW. TAKE YOUR PUPPIES WITH YOU," the patchwork stranger said to the werewolf Alpha, "OR STAY AND FIGHT ME YOURSELF."

He cracked his massive knuckles. The sound echoed up the hillside.

"On the full moon, when I'm at full strength, I'll make you pay for this," Coach Ewflower threatened. "I will personally rip you asunder, bone from bone, muscle from muscle. I'll suckle the meat from your sinew with a smile. You'll regret this."

"I REGRET NOTHING," the stranger said.

The coach retreated up the hill. She howled. The other men and women got up, slowly, many of them limping as they followed her up and out of sight.

"They're going to burn the rest of the wolfsbane," Will said. "We have to stop them."

"NO. YOU'VE DONE ENOUGH. GO HOME," said the stranger in a shaky voice before falling to one knee. Will realized he had been posturing, to appear tougher than he was. In truth, he was badly injured, bleeding all over. Only his blood was more black than red.

"You're hurt," Will said.

"I WILL HEAL. NOW GO HOME, WHERE YOU ARE SAFE."

"Nowhere in East Emerson is safe for us anymore," Will said, "not now that the coach knows who we are."

"YOUR HOMES ARE SAFE," the stranger said. "NO EVIL CAN COME IN UNINVITED. WE SAW TO THAT."

"*We* who?" Will asked. "Who are you?"

The stranger said nothing. He simply stared at Will with his different-colored eyes—one emerald green, the other yellow and black—then got up and walked away. Will followed.

At the bottom of the hill, tucked behind a curve of rock, the stranger approached the mouth of an old mine. It was locked up with iron gates and chains, covered in signs saying NO TRESPASSING and DANGEROUS and BEWARE CAVE-INS. But the stranger turned to the right and pressed in a stone set in an old rock wall.

A door slid aside.

"STOP FOLLOWING ME, WILL HUNTER," the stranger called. "TAKE YOUR FRIENDS AND LEAVE THIS PLACE. GO HOME. OESTRE IS DANGEROUS. SHE WILL NOT LET YOU LIVE IF SHE HEARS OF THIS."

"Tell me who you are. Please!"

The stranger hesitated. "ISN'T IT OBVIOUS? LOOK AT ME. I'M A MONSTER."

"Come on, Will." Ivy appeared behind him, pulling at his

shirt. "We need to get home before it gets dark, before Ewflower comes after us again."

Will hesitated and then called out, "You're not a monster. Monsters don't save people. Thanks for saving us. Again."

But the man disappeared into the dark tunnel without another word. As the door slid back into place, Will saw that one of the stones was marked with a large Roman numeral:

I

Another door, Will thought. Part of all the tunnels below East Emerson.

Did they all lead to Simon? What else was down there? And what would happen if Ozzie did bring back Simon? Would it be as bad as she had told him? Or would it be far worse?

Chapter 10
turkey interrupted

✳

"I have a good feeling," Ms. Vásquez said. "Today is going to be a wonderful day."

"I sure hope so," Will mumbled, feeling the exact opposite. He'd been plagued with a bad feeling ever since the run-in with Ewflower and her wolves at Viking's View.

Trusted Reader, if I haven't mentioned it before, you should always trust your gut. Your gut, also known as your belly or stomach, is the most sensitive organ in your body. Some might even say it's a little psychic. For instance, when I have beans, my gut says, "You're going to be farting later." And you know what? I always am.

"Do we have everything?" Mom asked.

Will checked the dishes balanced in his arms: "Elote, camote, fried polenta with chorizo, green bean casserole, and a chipotle–cream cheese pumpkin pie. Yup, that's everything."

"I can't believe you cooked all that by yourself," Mom said. "Lo hiciste bien, mijo."

"It isn't what I planned, but I think it works. I just hope it tastes like the ingredients cost more than twenty dollars."

Mom's lips thinned. "You did great with what we had. I'm sure it'll taste like a million bucks. I'm so proud of you, Guillermo. You did all this without your—"

Will interrupted, "Is it okay if we don't talk about him?"

"Of course," Mom said. She grabbed her keys and a mason jar of fresh flowers picked from their backyard. "Let's go."

Will stood in the road while Mom locked the front door. As Will adjusted the dishes in his arms, he noticed something he'd never seen before… He whispered, "No way." Carved on the front curb of his house was a coded message:

Hgvk lm gsrh kilkvigb zmw uliuvrg blfi oruv. Gszg'h irtsg. Gsrh slfhv rh fmwvi nb kilgvxgrlm.
—Lizxov Qlmvh

When Mom joined him to cross Ophidian Drive, he spotted another message carved into the curb of the Cross's home too. It said:

Gsrh slfhv gll.
Pvvk blfi xozdh gl blfihvou. Li vohv.
—L.Q.

"You okay?" Mom asked.

"Yeah, yeah, I'm fine," Will said. He couldn't wait to tell Ivy and Linus. He wondered if they knew about the messages.

Ms. Vásquez rang the doorbell. A moment later, the door opened to two men dressed in sweaters with turkeys on them. One was Mr. Cross. The second man Will had never seen before.

"Welcome! Come in, come in!" said Mr. Cross, taking the dishes from Will.

The second man took Ms. Vásquez's hand and said, "So nice to meet you." Then he turned to Will. "And you must be the brave young man who spends time with our rebellious children. I've heard so much about you."

"Who are you?" Will asked.

"I'm the *other* Mr. Cross. Well, Mr. Cross-Fayed. But you can call me Amir."

"Oh, yeah, you've met *Dad*, but not *Baba*," Ivy said. She was setting the table with Linus in the dining room. "Baba is our other dad."

"You have *two* dads?!" Will asked, an edge to his question.

"Affirmative," Linus said.

"You don't have a problem with that, do you?" Ivy growled defensively.

"Of course not!" Will snapped, thinking of his best friend, Marcellus, in Brooklyn, who had two moms.

Ms. Vásquez blushed. "Guillermo, you're embarrassing me. Explain yourself."

Everyone stared at Will.

His heart raced, his stomach ached, his lungs seemed to tighten. Will was uncomfortable and upset and sad and angry, all at the same time. He felt like he might explode...

Then he remembered Dina Iris's advice in the graveyard: to swallow his pride and confide in his friends.

"I'm not trying to be rude. I just... I usually spend today with my own dad. But since we moved here, he hasn't called me. Not even once." Will found it hard to breathe.

Admitting this to Ozzie in a cemetery in the dark was

easy. But now? In the light of day? In front of his friends? It made it too real. But Will forced himself to continue. "For a while now, I've been jealous of Ivy and Linus. Mr. Cross is always so nice and present and always offering us snacks. My dad can't even be bothered to let me know if he's alive. Or if he cares if I'm alive. And now I find out that Ivy and Linus have *two* dads—" Will's words stuck in his throat, but he pushed them out "—and I don't even have *one*."

Ms. Vásquez hugged her son.

"Is that why you've been such a total—" Ivy started.

Linus put his finger on his sister's lip. "Give our friend a moment."

"I'm sorry, Ivy," Will said. "You're one of my only friends here. I didn't mean to upset you. I just thought you were being rude to your dad, and I got, I guess, mad 'cause I was...jealous. Your dad, *both* your dads, must love you and Linus so much. I hope you know how lucky you are."

Ivy's eyes started to water. Then she crossed the distance to Will and looked him in the eye. "Of course I know how lucky I am. Being adopted is scary. But Linus and I ended up with two parents who love us. They treat me way better than I deserve."

"That's not true," Mr. Cross said. "You deserve all our love and more."

"Yeah, but Linus is all perfect, and I'm a total screwup."

"That's because you take after me," Mr. Cross-Fayed said. He grinned a mischievous smile, the way Ivy often did. Then he hugged Ivy. "We accept you as you are."

Mr. Cross hugged Linus. "We love both of you. No matter what you do."

"Let's see if that sticks when I end up in jail for battling witches and werewolves," Ivy muttered.

"You sound like Will," Ms. Vásquez said. "Always making up ridiculous stories."

"No wonder our kids get along," Baba said. All the parents laughed. Will, Linus, and Ivy exchanged knowing glances.

Ivy turned to Will again. "I'm sorry too. I know I can be a real jerk sometimes. I pretend not to care, but I do. I just don't want people to know. That's why I treat this goober like a goober." Ivy pushed Linus playfully.

Linus hugged his sister. "You could certainly prank me less, but you are a good sister. You shield me from terrible things all the time, be it bully or a vampire."

"Well, yeah. You're my little brother. It's my job to take care of you."

"See? You are a better person than you think, Ivy Bong-Cha."

"It means 'superior daughter,' which is fitting, since I am superior." Ivy playfully pushed Will.

Will smiled. "Are we good?"

"Yeah, we're good," Ivy said. Will, Ivy, and Linus all hugged.

Ms. Vásquez's eyes teared up.

Mr. Cross-Fayed said, "*Awww.* We have such great kids. Look at this outpouring of love and emotion. It's so perfectly in the spirit of being grateful and giving thanks."

"Yuck. Enough of all that junk," Ivy said, wiping her cheeks. "Where's the dead bird? I'm hungry, and I demand turkey slathered in gravy."

"Everyone take a seat," Mr. Cross said. "We'll bring out the rest of the food."

Baba said, "I'll help."

"So will I," Ms. Vásquez added.

As the parents disappeared into the kitchen, our three friends looked around the room, suddenly shy. You see, Friendly Reader, after someone has shown a more sensitive side, they are often embarrassed and feel quite raw. This was certainly the case with Will and Ivy.

Fortunately, they were surrounded by warmth and affection. Not just from each other and their parents, but by the beautifully set table full of diverse dishes. Will had brought food that reminded his mom of her abuela and Mexico. Ivy had made her Korean cornbread, and Linus his favorite, thrice-baked potatoes. Mr. Cross had made his cornbread stuffing, based on a recipe passed down from parent to child for generations. And Mr. Cross-Fayed had set out his falafel-spiced deviled eggs, pomegranate-cranberry sauce, and saffron roasted turkey.

Hungry Reader, you might think I am lavishing over the food for a bit too long, but I think it an important reminder that not every child is fortunate enough to have loved ones and a full meal on the holidays. Whether you have these things or not, know that you are not alone in your circumstances, and that circumstances often change. Early in my monstrous life, I spent many holidays alone. But now I am surrounded by friends, family, and my dog, Toby, who would bite any mail carrier who tried to interrupt my newfound happiness.

If you have a hard time with holidays—be it because of

a missing father, not enough to eat, or a town full of were-wolves who are stalking you—know that things can get better, and most likely, they will. Give it time.

I am done interrupting. Back to the story.

"I'm glad we got that out of the way," Ivy said. "I hated fighting with you, Will."

"Me too," Will said. "Sorry I was being such a weirdo."

"We're all weirdos," Ivy said.

"I concur." Linus smiled.

"Okay. Enough with this emo stuff. Let's move on. I guess I'll ask what we've all been avoiding: Is anyone else wigged about Ewflower knowing who we are?"

"Totally," Will admitted. "I could barely sleep last night. But on our way over, I saw codes on our curbs—just like the ones at the library. I think Oracle is protecting us against the Thirteen. They can't step on our property."

"Does that work for werewolves too?"

"I don't know."

"I also did not sleep last night. But I used the time to synthesize this." Linus held up a tiny vial. It contained a violet metallic fluid.

"What is it?"

"Concentrated essence of wolfsbane and liquid silver,"

Linus said. "It will either unmake a werewolf, or kill it. Unfortunately, it remains completely untested. At the very least, it will be a good form of last resort self-defense." He slid it into his pocket.

"Why last resort?" Ivy asked.

"Because I have no idea if it'll work."

"Well, here's to hoping we don't find out today. After all, it's a holiday," Ivy replied. "Surely werewolves take off for national celebrations. Don't they like eating food like the rest of us?"

"Halloween is a holiday, and Ozzie didn't take that off last month," Will noted.

"Well, let us stay optimistic in the face of adversity. We will enjoy ourselves today and worry about the fate of the town tomorrow," Linus stated. "Have I mentioned I am famished? I skipped eating breakfast today in lieu of the coming feast. I wanted to have as much room in my gastrointestinal tract as possible."

"Same here," Will said. He rubbed his temples. "I must be hungry—I'm starting to get a headache."

"You took Oracle's anti-wolf-command serum, right?" Ivy asked.

Will gulped. "I was so busy cooking, I forgot it on the counter… Maybe missing a dose is okay?"

"*No!*" Ivy and Linus both shouted.

They were up and at the door when Ms. Vásquez peeked out of the kitchen to ask, "Where are you going?"

"Oh, um… I forgot the salt and pepper," Will said.

"We have salt and pepper," Mr. Cross said.

"Take a seat, all three of you," Will's mom said.

"But I really need to—"

"Will. Stop acting strange. Siéntate."

Will sat. His head was spinning. He felt suddenly faint. As the adults disappeared back into the kitchen, Will whispered to his friends, "Can you hear her? Ewflower is in my head—"

"It's on your kitchen counter? I'll go get it," Linus said. He ducked out of the house and ran across the street.

"I can hear my alpha, clear as day—" Will grabbed his head, which was pounding. "She orders every man, woman, and child under her control to go to Ophidian Drive—"

Before Ivy's eyes, Will began to change further. The fur on his face grew thicker, flowing over his entire body. His fangs and claws lengthened, his ears perked upward, and his eyes turned blacker. He howled.

Ms. Vásquez called out from the kitchen, "Will, I understand you're hungry, but no need to be rude."

Will looked more like a werewolf than ever. He growled, "…must bite…" He shook his head. His eyes turned almost normal for a second as he said, "I can hear the Alpha in my head. You have to lock me up. Hurry!"

"Upstairs," Ivy said.

Ivy rushed Will up the stairs and into her room. Will had never been in here before. There was the expected mess of clothes and sports equipment, but what caught him off guard was a huge poster hanging on the wall. "Are those kittens?"

Before Ivy could respond, Will's eyes darkened and he roared, baring his teeth at them. "Bite!" he growled.

Luckily, Ivy was used to monster attacks by now and immediately leaped on him, trying to hold him down. She almost had him to the floor when Will shoved her off, kicking her across the room. Ivy slammed into the wall.

"Everything okay up there?" Mr. Cross called from downstairs.

"Yup! No need to come up!" Ivy shouted. "We're just, uh, doing some exercises before the feast to, um, help build up our appetites!"

Ivy jumped across the room, onto Will's back. Will spun in circles, trying to force Ivy off, but she refused to let go. She leaned back, hoping her weight would tip them over enough to knock him down.

Linus ran into the room, holding the potion. "I've got it!"

Ivy shouted, "Great. But we have to get him to drink it. Will's wolfing out!"

Linus wrapped his arms around Will's legs, hoping to knock him over. But Will fought with supernatural fury, kicking Linus off, then tossing Ivy onto the bed.

"Must bite!" Will grumbled through sharp teeth. But then he sniffed the air. "Mmmmm…food? Turkey?"

Will ran, bursting through Ivy's door, shattering it into a million pieces. He raced downstairs on all fours. Linus and Ivy chased after him. "No, no, no, no!"

They barely made it to the dining room in time to witness Will leap onto the table and attack the cooked turkey. He took one massive bite, then shook his head from side to side, flinging stuffing everywhere. He went from dish to dish, shoving his face into each, gobbling up the food as if he'd never eaten with silverware in his life. Mr. Cross, the other Mr. Cross, and Ms. Vásquez ran out of the kitchen and watched, horrified, as the meal was destroyed.

Mr. Cross shouted, "Our feast!"

Ms. Vásquez said, "What on earth?!"

"We can explain—" Linus started. But he didn't have to.

As you know, Smart Reader, East Emerson is the victim of a town curse. Any strange phenomenon that occurs cannot be seen by the people who are within the town's borders—unless they have the magical sight, like our three young detectives. Otherwise, their brains will see something different, something far more reasonable. So instead of seeing Will transformed into a werewolf destroying the Thanksgiving meal, the adults at the table saw something else entirely.

"It's a wild animal!" yelled Baba.

The adults, believing a wild dog was attacking their holiday feast, tried to stop Will. They grabbed at him, which is when Will did the unthinkable—*he bit them*.

"*Dad!*" Linus shouted.

"*Baba!*" Ivy screamed.

But it was too late.

Will had bit Mr. Cross, Mr. Cross-Fayed, and now, even his own mom. But the second he did, he seemed to realize in horror what he had done and the guilt of it shocked him back to himself.

"Drink this!" Linus said.

Will took the potion and swallowed it down. He was still a wolf, but he was no longer under the control of Ewflower.

He stared at his mom, clutching her bleeding forearm. "Mom! I'm so, so sorry… Are you… Are you okay?"

"I'm fine, sweetie. Just a little dog bite."

But she was not fine, Dear Reader. None of them were. As you have witnessed throughout our tale, werewolf bites act fast. This one followed accordingly. Ivy and Will watched helplessly as their parents began to transform. Furry, fanged, and black-eyed, Ms. Vásquez and both Mr. Crosses started to sniff the air.

"If we make it out of this alive, we should remember to start carrying doggie treats," Ivy said to her brother. The two of them backed away slowly. No sooner had they turned to run, when their fathers took notice. Both Mr. Crosses bounded across the room. Ivy and Linus barely made it to the stairs when they were grabbed from behind.

"Let us go, Dad!" Linus shouted.

"Baba, don't do this!"

"Sorry, kids," Mr. Cross said, "but our pack leader wants you."

Ms. Vásquez took hold of Will. "Same for you, young man."

"You can't!" Ivy argued. But it was too late. The three adults were all being mind-controlled. They pushed their children toward the front door.

"Mom, please! Don't do this," Will called out. "You'll regret it!"

"Regret it or not, I must do what Ewflower asks of me," Ms. Vásquez said. "She is my one true Alpha."

As our young trio of heroes were pushed outside into the daylight, they found the street full of werewolves, waiting at the curb. A small army had gathered on Ophidian Drive. Even if Dina Iris or Oracle Jones or the gray stranger were to come, there would be no rescue. There were simply too many people to fight.

Standing front and center was Coach Ewflower herself. With a sinister smile, she sneered. "You three have caused me a lot of problems. But no longer. Ready to meet your final fate?"

"Can we say no?" Will asked.

Ewflower glared. "I don't know how you're managing to disobey me, but you've only doomed yourself. Watch as your friends join my side."

The Alpha wolf ordered three of her largest werewolves

to step forward. "I should kill you for your insolence. Luckily for you, I need every hand on deck for what's next—even two willful brats such as yourselves. Men—bite the unbitten!"

"No!" Will cried, even as he was held in place by his mom.

"Stop!" Ivy shouted at her fathers.

Their parents seemed conflicted, wanting to both obey their Alpha and help their children. But they watched as two large werewolves stepped forward. One grabbed Ivy's arm. The other grabbed Linus's. Then: *CHOMP! CHOMP!*

"Ow!!" Ivy shrieked.

"That is unpleasant!" Linus added.

"Being turned isn't supposed to feel nice," Ewflower growled. "It's supposed to hurt. Wait until you start to grow fur and fangs and your bones reshape themselves to that of a total wolf on the full moon."

"Yeah, no thanks," Linus said.

"That's a hard pass for me too," Ivy added.

"Like you have a choice!" Ewflower laughed. "Any minute now you'll change, and you'll be subservient to me."

The pack leader watched. Everyone else did too. They stared at Ivy and Linus. Any minute now their transformations should begin. The wait continued. The coach looked at her watch. "Why aren't you changing?"

Linus grinned. He repeated the verse the lamia librarian had found: "'Petal of Wolf's Bane once a day, keeps the wolf at bay or away.'"

Ivy chuckled. "We've both been eating small amounts of wolfsbane since we found it. We're not turning into anything. And we're definitely not joining your army." Ivy and Linus high-fived each other. Will couldn't help but smirk at his friends.

"Sorry, Coach," Ivy added. "Looks like you've been outsmarted by kids."

Ewflower sneered. "All you've done is doom yourselves. You can join the others in the pyre."

"What's a pyre?" Ivy asked.

Linus answered, "A heap of combustible materials, usually used for fire and burning a corpse during a funeral ceremony."

"Whose funeral?" Will asked.

Ewflower grinned. "Yours."

Chapter 11
the New boss in town

✴

"Mom, you have to let us go," Will pleaded.

"Sorry, mijo, but we must do what the Alpha tells us," Ms. Vásquez said, her eyes as black as night.

"Dad, Baba, you can't do this," Ivy begged.

"But we have to. We must obey our pack leader," Mr. Cross said.

"They are going to kill us!" Ivy shouted.

The three parents seemed to hesitate—as if they were trying to fight the werewolf mind control. But it didn't last. The wolfen magic was too strong.

Will, Ivy, and Linus were hoisted into the air and carried by their parents alongside dozens of their neighbors, all of whom had been bitten. The army of werewolves marched after Coach Ewflower as she led them down toward the town square.

Dear Reader, when a large number of people turn against you all at once—whether at school or in a town mob—it is quite terrifying. I have faced many mobs in my day. Some threw stones. Some shot arrows or swung swords or chucked spears at me. Others came after me with the traditional set of pitchforks and torches. I have also had my fair share of axes, rifles, and crossbows aimed in my direction. Yet none are quite so frightening as the mobs on the internet. Those people say the cruelest things. Whenever I am attacked—online or in the flesh—I try to remember the adage "Sticks and stones may break my bones, but words will leave a lasting emotional scar on my psyche that years of expensive therapy will help but never truly vanquish."

Still, our three heroes were not concerned with psychological devastation and future mental health so much as they were worried about losing their lives. They were so afraid they felt like peeing their pants. Have you ever been that afraid? It's very uncomfortable for you *and* your bladder.

"Linus, Ivy, I'm so sorry for getting us into this mess," Will called to his friends over the mob carrying them.

"It is hardly your fault," Linus said. "You were bit saving me."

"Well, it's a little his fault for biting our parents," Ivy noted.

"Now is not the time to cast blame," Linus said. "Now is the time to figure out how to escape."

"Will, are you *you* again? Like really you?" Ivy asked.

"Yeah," Will said. "But I have no clue how to get us out of this. Linus, any ideas?"

"I am thinking. But I am open to your thoughts and concepts as well."

"Having a hard time focusing," Will said. "I'm kinda distracted by the angry mob carrying us to our doom—my mom among them."

Ivy shouted down at Dad and Baba, "Boy, are you two going to feel horrible if we die."

"We're not going to die," Will said. "We could still be rescued. Maybe by Dina Iris, or Oracle Jones, or the gray stranger—"

"They're not coming," Ivy said. "We need to figure out how to get out of this on our own."

"Wait, why is Coach taking us to a pyre?" Will asked. "What about Ozzie? Maybe we can say we need to talk to her?"

"What'll that do? Ozzie would kill us too."

"It'd buy us time," Will noted.

"Looks like we're out of time actually." Ivy nodded ahead to the center of the town square. A dozen werewolves formed a line from the hardware store to the pyre, each passing wood plank after wood plank toward a giant tower of piled wood.

"All this for us?" Ivy asked.

"No," Linus answered. "This is a witch burning."

"But we're not witches," Will said.

"No, but *she* is."

The crowd parted to reveal Ozzie herself—only the witch was gagged and bound in heavy chains. Both hands were covered in manacles so that she couldn't so much as snap her fingers. The chains were held in place by dozens of werewolves. The witch struggled to free herself from her bonds, but they held fast. Her face was bloodied and bruised and clawed.

The massive manacles that bound her had an inscription:

23-05 02-09-14-04 15-05-19-20-18-05'19 13-01-07-09-03,
06-18-15-13 08-01-18-13-09-14-07 20-08-05-19-05 03-
08-01-09-14-19,
15-18 08-01-18-13-09-14-07 15-20-08-05-18-19.

"Why is Ozzie chained up?" Ivy shouted at the coach. "I thought you worked for her?"

"There's been a change in management," Ewflower said, scowling. "The witch promised me belonging, equality, inclusivity. Instead, she treated me like a servant. Forced my new pack to dig out the tunnels below, like dogs."

"But why?" Ivy asked. "Ozzie's a witch. Why didn't she just magic away the dirt or something?"

Coach Ewflower grabbed Ozzie by the hair and growled into her face. "Because she's weaker than she lets on. That, and the labyrinth below is protected from sorcery, impervious to magical manipulation. The only way to dig it out is by hand. It would take centuries for one person to do it alone, so she used me. She used us—she used all of us." Ewflower indicated the werewolves all around. Everyone howled.

Nearby, something rattled in a small golden cage. It was Ozzie's familiar, Faust. The hare beat its dragon wings against the cage and hissed at the wolves, wanting to save its master.

Ozzie didn't make a sound. Yet in her piercing and pale purple eyes, Will saw something familiar—fear. But only for the briefest of moments. When Ozzie turned to Ewflower, her eyes seethed with fury and hatred.

The witch lunged at Ewflower, as though she might burst through her chains and strangle the werewolf with her bare hands. But the chains held, and Ozzie fell to her knees.

Ewflower smirked. "You may be tough, but you weren't ready for my ambush, were you? Sure, it took a hundred werewolves to take you down, but in the end, we did it. Not so powerful now, are you, witch?" Ewflower kicked Oestre in the ribs.

"Hey!" Will shouted. "She's already tied up, and you're about to burn her at the stake! No need to kick her when she's down."

The coach laughed. "If I didn't know better, I'd think you were on her side."

"No one deserves to be kicked around," Will said.

The Alpha werewolf ignored him and addressed her pack. "Tie these three kids up with the others!"

As Linus, Ivy, and Will were brought forward, they saw two more prisoners: Ms. Delphyne and Mr. Villalobos. Will's heart sank. "What are you doing here?"

"I'm a natural-born werewolf," Mr. Villalobos explained. "I'm not part of Ewflower's pack. When she gave me the option to serve her, I refused."

"For that, he must be put to death," Ewflower stated.

"And the librarian?" Linus asked, concern written in his eyes.

"I'm his fiancée," Ms. Delphyne said.

"You two are engaged?" Linus asked in disbelief.

"We are, and happily so." Ms. Delphyne smiled as she wiggled her ring finger. "Didn't you ever notice the rock on my finger?"

Despite more important concerns, Linus felt frustrated. He wasn't sure if this came from a scientific point of confusion or from his crush on the caretaker of books. "Aren't you two different species?"

"It doesn't matter. We're in love," Ms. Delphyne said, placing her forehead against Mr. Villalobos's. "What can I say, I love a mathematician."

"Good for you," Ivy said sincerely.

"I know math," Linus whispered.

"Enough!" Ewflower roared. "This is not some foolish reality show about finding monster love. This is the start of my wolfen crusade! Now tie those three up with the others."

Will, Ivy, and Linus were shoved past the librarian and the math teacher and escorted to two new stakes. Ivy and Linus were bound, back-to-back, with rope. Will was tied to the last stake alone, next to Ozzie.

Werewolves pounded Ozzie's chains into the ground with massive iron nails and sledgehammers. She fought to free herself, but even with her magical strength, she couldn't budge. Then the werewolves began to pile wood and kindling all around them.

Ewflower took the stage of the town square gazebo. "Hello, my darling wolves. How are we tonight?!"

The mob cheered. "*Wooo!*"

"*We're great!*"

"*Let's kill us some witches!*"

"Okay, okay, we'll get there. Settle down now," Coach Ewflower said. "First, let's chat. You know who I am? Lacy Ewflower, born right here in East Emerson. Grew up here, went to school here, became an Olympic-level athlete here. And after winning a medal for my country, I came home and led our school district sports teams to win state *and* nationals three years in a row!"

The mob cheered again, calling out, *"Coach! Coach! Coach!"*

"And you know what? I didn't even get a raise. Then my husband took my kids and left—said I cared more about sports than my family. You know what he left me with? Nothing but a mortgage and a bunch of trophies. I was down on my luck—until Oestre here brought me into her coven of Thirteen. Said she needed a real leader, a coach like me, to help build an army. She promised me a family. But she didn't deliver."

"Boo!" the crowd hissed.

"Then I realized…with all of you, I have built more than a pack. I've built a *family.*"

Will gazed at Ivy and Linus. The crowd around them chanted and whistled and clapped. *"Coach! Coach! Coach!"*

"Oestre wanted all of you to do her bidding, to dig up the tunnels below East Emerson. But I have a different plan, a new vision for our werewolf pack. We will take over this and the neighboring towns, turning every single person into one of us. Then on the night of the full moon, when we all become full wolves, we will take over the state of Massachusetts. Then on the next full moon, we'll take over the nation. And eventually, we'll take over the world!!"

The mob hooted and hollered and howled, like they were at the best sporting event of their life. As the sun set on the western horizon, Will noticed the sky looked like it was on fire. Some tug in his gut worried this was a premonition, that he would be on fire soon.

Ewflower lit a torch and held it high in the air. The crowd went wild.

Ivy called out to Will, "Is it just me or is this the worst pep rally of all time?"

"It is," Will called back. "It's not real pep if you're being mind-controlled."

"I have never enjoyed pep rallies," Linus added.

"So…" Ivy started. "Our situation looks pretty bad, right? We're tied to stakes, surrounded by half the town, all of them werewolves under Ewflower's Alpha command. Even if we got free, we couldn't battle this crowd."

"You're right," Will said. "There's only one person strong enough to do that."

"Who?" Linus asked.

Will nodded to his left, to the bound witch. "Ozzie."

She looked at Will incredulously.

"Will, she's the bad guy," Ivy said.

Ignoring his friend, Will spoke directly to Ozzie. "Whatd'ya say, Ozzie? If we free you, will you help us take down Ewflower and free our parents?"

The witch glared at Will.

"I know, I know, you're supposed to be all tough and terrifying," Will said. "But that night in the cemetery, I saw you. I saw the *real* you: a woman who's done some questionable things because she's in love with someone. Ewflower is full of hate and anger. But you? You're capable of love. You spoke to me with kindness. Yeah, I know you're supposed to be the villain, but deep down, I think you're a good person, Oestre."

The witch hesitated.

"Will you help us?"

Ozzie closed her eyes, breathed through her nose, then finally…nodded.

"But I want you to promise me: you won't hurt us after."

Reluctantly, the witch nodded again.

"You have lost your dang mind, Will Hunter," Ivy said. "Not that any of it matters, since we're still tied up. If we're not free, how do we free Ozzie?"

"Do you have the athame?"

"The what now?"

"The silver dagger that Oracle gave you?"

"Yeah! I learned my lesson last time. It's in my boot," Ivy said. "But I can't reach it."

"Linus, wiggle in the ropes. Ivy, try to bring your boot up, so your brother can squat down. If he can reach the dagger, he can cut you free. You have to hurry, though, while the coach is distracted with her pregame speech."

"Boy, that woman can talk," Ivy said. "She's still going! A little full of herself, huh?"

"Gives us more time to escape," Will replied.

As Linus struggled to get the blade from Ivy's boot, the entire crowd fixated on their pack leader's every word. Ewflower loved the attention, and couldn't help but talk and talk and talk.

Quiet Reader, lots of people desperately crave this kind of attention. I do not. Though I very much appreciate my readers reading that which I've written, please know and understand, I do *not* crave attention. In fact, I despise it. It gives me anxiety. Who wants everyone staring at them? Certainly not me. Growing up, any time I had attention, it was because I had fallen, or been bullied or mocked, or made a fool of myself…which I did quite often because I am quite clumsy. My point is, attention is terrifying. I would much rather be left alone so I can write more stories for you. So please, stop staring at me so I can get back to our tale…

"I have it!" Linus said. He pulled the dagger from Ivy's boot and lifted it. Carefully, he started sawing through their ropes.

"Hurry it up," Ivy said. "Miss Talkative is wrapping up her speech."

"I am trying! Do you know how thick these ropes are? Why did Oracle not give us a sharper blade?" Linus asked in frustration. "Will, it's going to be a few minutes."

"I don't know if we have that long. After you free yourself, you have to free Ozzie."

"With everyone watching?" Ivy asked. "We need a distraction."

"Like what?" Will asked.

"Challenge her," Ivy said. "A fight to become Alpha. The last werewolf rule, remember? The only way to become the new Alpha is to kill the old Alpha."

"I can't kill her!" Will gulped. "And I can't fight her either. I'll lose!"

"You don't have to win. You just have to keep her distracted long enough for us to get Ozzie free."

Will's head spun. He'd never won a fight before. Heck, he'd never been in a fight before. Unless you count video games.

Will looked at Ivy and Linus. He looked at his math teacher and the librarian. He looked at Ozzie. Then at his mom, standing between Ivy and Linus's fathers. Will gazed out over the crowd of the town, all of them werewolves, hanging on every word coming out of Coach Ewflower's mouth. It wasn't just his life at stake—it was everyone's in East Emerson.

Will wondered what his dad would do…

His dad would probably just leave. Take care of himself. Not worry about anyone else. Not bother to return their calls.

Well, Will didn't want to be like his dad. Will didn't need his dad to be strong. Will had a new family, a new pack—Ivy and Linus. And he wasn't going to let them down.

Will dug deep down, feeling his werewolf strength. His claws grew, and he slashed through the ropes binding him to the stake. He jumped off the pyre, stomped forward, shoving adults twice his size out of the way. He leaped ten feet into the air, over the rest of the crowd, and onto the gazebo stage.

"Coach Ewflower!" Will bellowed. "I challenge you!"

The Alpha took him in, her eyes roaming from his toes to his head. She laughed. "Challenge me to what?"

"Trial by combat. Whoever wins becomes the new Alpha of the East Emerson pack."

Everyone in the crowd began laughing. The roar of laughter rose. Even Ewflower was having a good guffaw.

"Oh, no," Ivy whispered to Linus, "we have to hurry."

"I am hurrying," Linus said, struggling to cut the thick ropes faster, despite his hands being tied behind his back. "It would have been easier if he had let us go before storming off."

"This was a bad plan," Ivy whispered. "Will can't win this. He's dead meat."

"It is a good plan, Ivy," Linus said. "Or at least, it's the only plan we had."

Back on the gazebo stage, Ewflower stepped forward, towering over Will. "Don't be ridiculous," the Alpha werewolf shouted at Will in front of the crowd. "You're barely a wolf pup. I would destroy you."

"You won't," Will said. "A good friend once told me that

in a battle of brains versus brawn, 'a logical mind will win every time.'"

"You're a fool to believe that," Ewflower said. "But I'm feeling generous. I'll give you one chance to step down."

"No, thank you," Will said. "I'm here to rumble."

"Good," Ewflower said, tossing the lit torch to the ground. She flexed, baring her wolfen muscles, her razor-sharp teeth, and her extended claws. She let out a roar that swept through the crowd. Will's whole body shivered.

The coach smiled. "You know, I've been craving a good fight for a while—especially one *to the death*."

Chapter 12
Battle for the Pack

✴

"Maybe we should rethink this?" Will suggested. "No one needs to die."

"Rules are rules," Coach Ewflower said with a fanged smile, her eyes as black as the darkest shadow. She stood opposite him on the gazebo, which was surrounded by hundreds of townspeople, including Will's mom.

"But rules are meant to be broken," Will squeaked.

"Not in sports, and not with werewolves," Ewflower growled. "I don't know how you broke my mental commands, but now I have to make an example of you. Are you ready?"

"To fight? No. To die? Even less so." Will gulped. What was he thinking? Ewflower was an adult, an athlete, and a werewolf pack Alpha. He was a middle schooler who liked to read comics and play video games. How could he possibly win in a fight against her?

"No more hesitation," Ewflower shouted to the cheering crowd. "Let the fight begin… NOW!"

Ewflower leaped across the stage. Will recalled the only move in gym class dodgeball that he'd ever mastered. He dodged, rolling to the right.

Will shouted, "To be fair, I don't like the idea of hitting a woman."

"That's sexist," Ewflower growled. "You should be prepared to hit anybody who stands in your way. But feel free to not hit me—I'm more than willing to have a flawless victory."

She vaulted again, this time swiping her paws to the right when Will tried to dodge. Her claws dug into his shoulder. He howled in pain as blood smeared his shirt.

"Will!" Ivy and Linus screamed.

Will had never heard so much ache in their voices. He couldn't let them down. They were his first friends in East Emerson. They laughed together, they made him smile, and they always had his back in their adventures. He had never had friends like them before, and he had to do whatever he could to give them a chance.

He charged at Ewflower.

Meanwhile, Ivy yelled at her brother, "Get us out of these ropes, Linus! Now! We have to help Will!"

"Almost done," Linus said, sawing as fast as he could while the werewolf mob watched the fight. His brow was pouring sweat as he tried not to think about Ms. Delphyne, her fiancé, Ozzie, and the kindling that surrounded them. All it would take was a spark from one of the lit torches, and up they'd go in flames. He had to hurry.

Ewflower dodged Will's charge. Now they paced opposite one another in a large circle. Will was trying to stay as far away from her as possible. Each time the pack leader attacked, Will dodged. She barked in frustration, "You can't keep this up forever."

"I know," Will said. "But I'm hoping you'll wear yourself out."

"Unlikely," she said. Will thought of a defense move from a video game. As Ewflower sprang at him, he rolled onto his back and kicked her overhead, using her momentum against her. She flew over the gazebo rail, crashing into the crowd. People hooted and hollered.

"I can't believe that worked!" Will muttered.

Ewflower stood, more furious than ever. "You'll die for that."

"I hope not," Will said, dodging the next swipe of her claws as she leaped back into the ring.

On the other side of the crowd, Linus finally cut through the ropes and they dropped away. He and Ivy were free. For the first time, he noticed odd letters carved into Oracle's dagger:

Gsv Lizxzorzm Yozwv.
(Ru olhg, kovzhv ivgfim gl Lizxov qlmvh. Gszmc!)

Ivy snatched the silver blade from his hand. "I have to help Will!"

Linus grabbed her. "Ivy, wait! They can't see that we are free! We have to follow Will's plan. We need Ozzie."

"No way. That witch is going to betray us as soon as we let her go. My friend comes first," Ivy snapped.

Linus held her arm. "Ivy, please, trust me. Trust the plan."

Ivy looked between her friend and her brother. There was no right decision. "Ugh. Fine! I'll give you sixty seconds. Clock starts ten seconds ago."

As Ivy and Linus worked to free Ozzie from her chains, Will counted his wounds. His right arm and left leg were bleeding. Claw marks covered his back and shoulders. And he was certain he'd lost enough blood to pass out very soon. He peered over the crowd at his friends. They were trying to free Ozzie. So it was up to Will to keep Ewflower distracted just a little longer. Maybe talking…

"Coach Ewflower. Rather than take over the town, have you considered a career in doggie day care? I feel like that might be a better use of your skill set."

"Stop playing with me, boy. Let's finish this," the pack leader growled. She hurtled toward Will. This time, he used a move he'd seen in a comic book. He stepped to the side and tripped her. The Alpha broke through the gazebo rail and bowled into the crowd. When she got up, she howled, and Will could hear her mental commands at the edge of his mind. *"Bring the boy to me!"*

Several large wolves hopped up on stage and pushed him into East Emerson's town square, so that he and Ewflower were surrounded by snarling wolves. Those behind shoved him forward, shrinking the circle and pushing him toward the Alpha pack leader.

"You can't use your mind control on the crowd," Will shouted. "That's cheating."

"I'm the pack leader. I can do whatever I want."

"These chains aren't coming off," Ivy snapped at Linus. "They must be magically binding or something."

"We have to break this lock," Linus said, hitting it with a rock.

"*Mmmmm-mmmm*," Ozzie murmured through the gag in her mouth.

Ivy looked back at Will. He was cornered by Ewflower, and she was closing in on him. "Sorry, Linus. Clock is up."

Ivy grabbed the blade from Linus's hand and stole the silver-wolfsbane concoction from his pocket. Then she forced her way through the crowd. As she got to the inner circle, two large men grabbed her. One held her arm, the other her waist. She couldn't break free. "Will!" she screamed. She kicked one of the werewolves in the face, then used her throwing arm to hurl the dagger and potion, calling out, "Will! Catch!"

Now, Dear Reader, as you might have noticed—Ivy threw a bladed weapon. If someone throws a knife at you and yells "catch," I would recommend *not* catching it, as you will likely end up with a knife sticking out of your hand. Of course, Will was not privy to the advice I have just given you. Instead, he leaped into the air and caught the blade—luckily—by the handle. His other hand caught the glass vial with the purple metallic potion. In video games, we call this a "Level Up," because Will was now ready to battle the boss.

Will winked at Ivy, and she smiled back. If he wasn't so terrified, he might have chuckled. Because he knew what he should do.

As Will landed, Ewflower vaulted forward. This time, Will dove down, rolled between her legs, and slammed the silver dagger through her tail and into the ground.

Ewflower howled louder than any wolf had before. A knife through the tail would have been painful enough, but the silver in the dagger was poisonous to her kind.

She tried to attack Will, but he was just out of reach, and the dagger held her in place. "I'll murder you for this!" she screamed.

"You were going to do that anyways," Will said. "But I don't want to kill you. Or anybody for that matter. Please, just give up. Release the title of Alpha to me, and I'll let everyone go—even you."

"*Never!*" Ewflower cried. She ripped the blade out of her tail and tossed it aside. "One of us will die here today, foolish boy. And it won't be me."

Ewflower bounded over and tackled Will to the ground.

She opened her mouth, her fangs shining, spit flying, ready to devour his face. Will winced, desperately thinking, *I hope this works.*

He uncapped the vial of silver liquid and purple flower petals and shoved it into the back of Ewflower's throat. The shock made her swallow.

The Alpha werewolf crashed backward. She clutched at her throat, as though suffocating. Her whole body fell into a massive seizure. There was the sound of bones breaking and reforming, muscles tearing, sinew shifting. She shrieked and shook as the points of her ears shrank, changing to soft curves. The fur fell away from her face and arms. Her fangs and claws retracted. And the black of her eyes dimmed to a light blue.

"What did you do to me?!" she asked.

"I killed you," Will stated. "At least, I killed the *wolf* part of you."

"How?!" she wailed.

"Teamwork," Will said, looking across the crowd at Linus, who gave a thumbs-up.

Ewflower's seizures stopped a minute later. She cried, "I'm… I'm…"

"Human," Will finished. "You're no longer the Alpha. *I* am."

All around Will, the werewolves bent their knees and bowed.

"Don't do that," Will said. "Stop that. Please. Everyone get up."

All of the werewolves obeyed. Some said, "Yes, sir. Whatever you say, sir." But as one of the werewolves stood, he accidentally kicked the torch lying on the cement sidewalk. It spun off to the side and into the kindling surrounding the stakes.

A blaze went up, racing toward the piles of wood around Ms. Delphyne, Mr. Villalobos, and Ozzie. Even as the fire roared around Linus, he didn't leave the witch. "How do I get you free?!" he shouted as the flames bit at his ankles.

Ozzie shouted *"mmmmm!!"* through her gag. Finally, Linus realized he didn't need to unlock Oestre's chains. He just needed to give her access to her magic—her voice. He yanked the gag out of her mouth.

"Enodnu si gnidnib eht, tlem sniahc eht!" the witch cried. There was a blast of violet light, and her chains melted away. She flew up into the air, shouting, *"Meht esaeler!"* Faust's cage fell apart and the hare flew free. The ropes fell from the lamia and her fiancé. Ms. Delphyne grabbed

Linus as her husband leaped to a safe distance away from the flames. The stakes were on fire, but no one was tied to them anymore.

Over the gazebo, a maelstrom whipped around Ozzie, dusting her off and pushing the nearby townspeople away with vast gusts of wind. Everyone was scattered and blown away, except one. "*Ewflower!*"

"You're too late, Ozzie," Ivy laughed, hugging Will. "My best bud took care of it."

"I couldn't have done it without you." Will smiled.

Lightning slashed the sky, slamming into the ground in front of Ewflower. Sparks sprayed the air. Ozzie waved her fingers and said, "*Etacoffus lliw uoy, em erofeb!*" An invisible force jerked Ewflower ten feet above the ground, where she clawed at her neck, unable to draw breath. Her legs kicked the air beneath her.

Ozzie's eyes burned red. "You made a dire mistake crossing me, Ewflower. I will snuff out your life as you would have done mine—"

"Wait!" Will shouted. He ran forward, waving his arms at the witch. "She's human again. She can't hurt anyone anymore. You don't have to kill her."

Ozzie hesitated. Ewflower's face was turning red from

lack of oxygen. Finally, she said, "*Og reh tel.*" The invisible force dropped Ewflower. The coach crashed to the ground and gasped for breath. "You are right, child. I won't kill her."

Will sighed a deep breath of relief. Ewflower was evil, but he didn't want her dead. He didn't want anyone to die. "Thank you."

"No, thank you…" Ozzie said, "…for the excellent idea. Death is too good for this Judas wolf. Instead, she'll be made to suffer for her betrayal. I will torture her with dark magic for years to come, until she *begs* me to kill her."

"No!" Will shouted, "Stop! You don't have to hurt people."

The witch looked at him, her face all fury.

"Ozzie. Oestre. Please. I know you're hurting, but you can't take it out on other people. Lashing out, being cruel, it doesn't accomplish anything. It just makes you feel more alone. No one wants to hang out with someone who kills people all the time."

Ozzie's eyes met Will's. Her face softened for the briefest of moments.

Then Ewflower spit at Will. "Don't defend me. I don't want your help. I don't need you. I don't need any of you!"

The gentleness in Ozzie's face drained away, turning to scorn. "The coach couldn't have said it better. I do not need you. And I do not want your help. You know nothing of me, Will Hunter. If you did, you would shudder and wet yourself in my presence—because I *am* evil, at its purest. And, yes, I know who you are now. You and your friends, Ivy and Linus Cross."

Will looked to his friends. They were as scared as he was.

"The three of you saved me the trouble of dealing with a wolf uprising. For that I am momentarily grateful. So I will keep my word. You freed me. So I'll allow you to free these people from the Wolf's Curse. You can renounce the beast, and all will be as it was. But the price for my grace is Ewflower's life."

Faust landed on Ozzie's shoulder, and the witch descended until she stepped onto the ground. She walked past the flames and toward a darkened street. With a snap of her fingers, something took hold of Ewflower and dragged her along behind the witch by her ankles, as if by an invisible rope.

"No! No, please!" Ewflower cried, her hands grabbing at the ground. But no matter what she clutched, grass or dirt or tree branch, the invisible force yanked her forward. The whole town watched, no one moving forward to help.

Only Will ran after. He leaped in front of Ozzie. "Don't do this! You're better than this!"

"I am not," Ozzie sneered. She backhanded Will, sending him sprawling across the grass. He sat up, holding his bleeding nose. Ivy and Linus rushed to his side.

"You have crossed me twice now, children. Meddle in my affairs one more time, and I will snap your necks with my bare hands. Consider this your *final* warning."

The witch took to the sky with her hare and her prisoner. They flew up and away, until they were consumed by the dark of night.

Ivy and Linus helped Will to stand. The three of them looked back. The fire from the stakes leaped onto the town square gazebo. And the townspeople, all of them still werewolves, stood there, waiting for orders from their new Alpha: Will.

The three friends looked at one another absently. They wanted to celebrate their victory. They'd saved East Emerson…again. But what was winning a single battle worth, if you still had to fight a war?

Chapter 13
~~the end~~ not the end

✳

The next morning, Will woke with Fitz licking his face. It took a full minute to realize that the dog's rough tongue was pressed against his skin. The fur was gone.

Will smiled.

He scratched the Saint Bernard behind the ears. Surveying his room, Will half expected to see a dangerous demon, a radioactive robot, a murderous maenad, or just a ghastly ghost come to haunt and taunt him with some new nightmare. He was glad that wasn't the case. There were no monsters, myths, mad science, or magic creatures there—not at the moment anyway. It was just Will and his dog.

He breathed a sigh of relief.

Downstairs, he found Mom sipping coffee at the kitchen table. "Good morning, mijo. How'd you sleep?"

"Like a very tired rock," Will said.

"Good, good…" Mom scratched her head, as if trying to recall something. "Will… Um, I'm having a hard time recalling yesterday… I know we sat down to Thanksgiving dinner with the Cross family, but then… I'm drawing a blank."

"Yesterday?" Will's mind went back to last night, after they defeated Ewflower, and Ozzie left with her…

Will did it. His first—and last—act as Alpha of the East Emerson werewolf community was to tell everyone to go home, forget anything weird that had happened in the last month. As far as anyone would recall, everyone had a nice Thanksgiving.

After that, Ms. Delphyne taught Will the ancient ceremony to "renounce the beast." Will spent an hour howling at the moon, until his ears and claws and teeth returned to normal. The black from his eyes was replaced with the usual white and brown, and his whole body went back to being smooth instead of furry. The only hair he had was in the usual places. He was a werewolf no more.

In fact, everyone returned to their proper selves. There were no more werewolves in East Emerson—except for Mr. Villalobos, who was born that way, and was also still allergic to himself. He was harmless—and head over heels in love with Ms. Delphyne. He kept following her around all night, asking if she was okay or had any splinters from being tied to the stake. Ivy and Will thought it was romantic. Linus was jealous.

As the townspeople left the town square, their memories erasing themselves, Mr. Villalobos said, "You three kids saved my fiancée. As far as I'm concerned, you all made an A in my math class for the rest of the year."

Ivy shouted, "Yes! Finally! Doing good pays off!"

Linus said, "Thank you for that, Mr. Villalobos, but we could not possibly accept such an offer. Grades must be earned. We were only doing what is just and morally correct. If you truly want to repay us, please keep all of this a secret from... well, whoever."

"Consider it done," Mr. Villalobos said.

"Nooooooo!" Ivy moaned.

"Thank you, for everything," the librarian added. "If you ever need research, don't hesitate to come to me. You saved my math man, my life, and the town. I am in your debt." With that, she kissed Linus on the cheek. He blushed so hard, he almost fell over.

After that, the three heroes came home, cleaned up the dining room, ate some of the pie that Will hadn't demolished, and watched cartoons. They were asleep before midnight.

"Will?" Ms. Vásquez said. Will was back in his kitchen, and his mom was waiting for an answer. "What happened yesterday?"

Will hated lying to his mom, so he decided to tell her the truth. "I turned into a werewolf, bit you and both of Ivy and Linus's fathers, turning all of you into werewolves, then Ivy, Linus, and I were almost burned at the stake along with a lamia librarian, a math teacher, and a witch. Then I had to fight the Alpha werewolf and take her place. But don't worry, us three kids saved the town. Again."

Mom squinted her eyes as if Will were a book with very tiny print…

…then she laughed. "Will, you have the oddest sense of humor."

Whether it was Will's mental commands or the town curse, Will wasn't sure, but Mom let it go. That was that.

Ms. Vásquez kissed her son on the forehead as she went to refill her coffee. "I know being in East Emerson, and being broke, and spending the holidays with your friends is all new, and it's not tradition. I know you would have preferred if your dad had been there, but… Well, I hope yesterday was a good day for you."

"It was," Will whispered. "I mean, do I miss Dad? Sure. But I called him a thousand times. He never called back. I'm done chasing him. Because you know what? I'm surviving. And I'm doing it without him. If he's not going to make me a priority in his life, then I'm not going to make him one in mine. He moved on with his life. Now I need to do the same thing."

"I think that's a very mature way to look at it." Ms. Vásquez added, a little sadness in her voice, "But I'm sorry you have to go through these complex feelings at such a young age. You should be living a carefree life, just being a kid."

Will almost laughed. "Trust me, being a kid is a lot harder than you think. Plus, I'm dealing with a lot scarier stuff these days."

"Like what?" Mom asked.

"You know, the usual. Witches. Werewolves. Maybe the end of the world."

His mom laughed. "Oh, Will. I love your imagination."

Will smiled to himself.

💀💀💀

That afternoon, Will met Ivy and Linus to walk over to the town square. They ordered three hot chocolates from the Cuco Café and sat outside in the cool autumn weather. They watched as bewildered police officers and firefighters tried to figure out why the gazebo had burned down. No one could recall anything.

"Cheers to us," Will said, holding up his mug to his friends. "We did it."

"Look at us, winning the day," Ivy said. "That's two victories under our belt."

"Yeah, well, I'm okay if that was the end of it," Will said. "I'd be fine if I never saw Ozzie or Oracle Jones or Dina Iris ever again."

"But if we only conquered two of the Thirteen," Linus noted, "logic and math would dictate we have eleven more to go."

"Not if we defeat Ozzie," Ivy said. "She's in charge. We stop her, we stop all of them…right?"

"Maybe if we asked her nicely enough," Will said.

The three of them laughed.

Will finally said, "I feel bad about Ewflower. I think she

was just really lonely after her divorce. She needed to feel loved. I get that. I've been a wreck because my dad wouldn't call me back. But after this month? It made me realize: I don't need him. I have my own pack—my mom, Fitz, and the two of you."

"That's sweet," Ivy said. "Totally corny, but sweet."

All three friends put their hands in for a fist bump.

Linus was the first to break the pleasant quiet. "Do you really think we can save East Emerson?"

"*You and danger have not parted; the next event's already started*," said a familiar, lyrical voice behind them. It was Dina Iris Grave, the silver fox. "*Prepare yourselves: the dead will walk again. You must be ready, this town you must defend.*"

"Can you ever bring us good news?" Will asked.

The fox smiled. "*In the distant past, soldiers fought alone——and ended up less than ash and bone. But now there are three, warmhearted and brave; together they'll work for the town to save. Though East Emerson's danger is far from gone, with you as its heroes, I'm sure we'll see dawn.*"

"That's not much to go on," Ivy said.

"On the contrary," Linus added. "It is hope."

"Well…" Will said, "…hope is certainly a good start."

a brief adieu

To my Dearest Reader,

Despite my warnings, you read this terrifying book and somehow managed to survive. Accolades to you. Congratulations. I tip my hat to thee, good sirs, madams, and persons.

The thought of such an incredible feat makes me almost feel alive. Admittedly, it is hard to know if one is alive or dead when they have died and been brought back to life as many times as I have. No matter, we should be celebrating that you still draw breath.

You ignored my sage advice and went forward and read the vicious accounts of what occurred in East Emerson to the likes of three children who are something like yourself: loyal, brave, intelligent, and beyond all, resilient. Oh, and yes, also doomed.

Please. If I ever write another book–DO NOT READ IT. It is for your own good and safety. It's all unintelligible scribble, dribble, and quibble anyway. No substance. Unless of course you like stories of the supernatural.

No! Ignore me. Don't read my stories. Please. I beg of you...

Sincerely, and WORST,
yours darkly,

-Adam Monster

p.s.

I lied.

Please read my books! I like scaring you! And I like scaring me! Every time I write down the true stories of East Emerson, I am terrified too.

And as Dina Iris Grave mentioned, things are not over. We still have more steps to take together. Will you be joining me for more? Please say no. I have grown rather fond of you, and would like to see you continue your life in the land of the living.

Why do you keep saying yes?! Who are you that you are so much stronger and braver than most—including me? Dearest Reader, how you bring me to tears by wanting to read my awful writing. But please, save yourself some fear. Here are three reasons to NOT pick up the third book in this series as soon as possible:

💀💀💀

#1. Because I am a *monster*. You should not trust monsters. And I told you *not* to read the next book. So if you should not read the next book, and you should not trust me, then you should read the next book. Sound logic indeed.

#2. Because you have uncovered the answer to several of our heroes' questions. Why continue on—even if you have more questions? You don't need to know what lies beneath East Emerson, do you? I mean, I plan on revealing more in the third book. Perhaps all. I don't know. Come if you want answers.

#3. And last but not least, because the upcoming book contains *even more monsters, more myths, more magic, more mad science,* and *more about the mystery of the strange, odd,* and *eerie East Emerson.* (There will also be more codes, ciphers, and cryptograms for you to figure out...)

Are you certain you're up for it?

Despite my concerns for you, I suspected you would be. Rest up, human childling, and sleep well...if you can. You will need your strength in the days and nights ahead. For the worst is yet to come...

p.p.s.

Do you know what an anagram is? You should probably look it up. I love anagrams. My story is full of them...

p.p.p.s.

Wahbyc adreef ygohui sjtkillmln roepaqdrisntgu?
Yvowux wyaznatb acndoetfhgehri cjokdlem? Sneor-
piqorusstluyv?!
Wwexlylz, laebtc mdee afsgkh yiojuk tlhminso.
Hpaqvres ytouuv fwixgyuzraebdc oduetf wghhoi Ij
akml ymento?
Tphqer asntsuwvewrx iysz raibgchdte ifng fhrio-
jnktl omfn yoopuq...
Sreset yuovuw sxoyozna!

* * * * *